"We can't stay here long or they'll figure out where we went."

Grasping the edge of the truck bed, Kaitlin straightened enough to peek over it. "So far, so good. Nobody followed us."

"What now?"

"We steal a getaway car."

"What?" Daniel's gaping jaw snapped shut when he heard her chuckle.

"Relax." Kaitlin grinned. "This is my truck. All I need is the keys and we can take off."

"Where are they?"

"In my purse. In your room."

His shoulders slumped. "My room?"

"Yes, but I know other ways in. Don't try anything funny while I'm gone. I'll be back in a jiffy."

Daniel grabbed her wrist to stop her. "Be careful."

"I will. Wait right there."

He watched her for as long as he could, then hunkered down in the chair. Kaitlin had to make it. She had to come back to him in one piece.

Sighing, he closed his eyes and prayed for exactly that.

Valerie Hansen was thirty when she awoke to the presence of the Lord in her life and turned to Jesus. She now lives in a renovated farmhouse on the breathtakingly beautiful Ozark Plateau of Arkansas and is privileged to share her personal faith by telling the stories of her heart for Love Inspired. Life doesn't get much better than that!

Visit the Author Profile page at Harlequin.com for more titles.

MARKED FOR REVENGE

VALERIE HANSEN

HARLEQUIN® LOVE INSPIRED® SUSPENSE

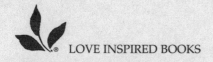

LOVE INSPIRED BOOKS

Recycling programs
for this product may
not exist in your area.

ISBN-13: 978-1-335-67913-0

Marked for Revenge

Copyright © 2019 by Valerie Whisenand

www.Harlequin.com

Printed in U.S.A.

Create in me a clean heart, O God;
and renew a right spirit within me.
–Psalm 51:10

To my children and grandchildren who put in long hours
helping others, both in emergencies and in hospitals.
I'm so proud of you all! And to my Joe,
who led the way and is still with me in spirit.

ONE

Fog filled the valley in the Ozarks. Icy morning air chilled off-duty police officer Daniel Ryan to the bone. He'd been sent to the remote, deserted homestead for his own safety, or so his chief had claimed, but he knew there would be no true escape for him. Ever. Too much had happened.

He tensed. Real threats could lurk out there in the fog. Assassins. Armed and deadly. He could almost see them, sneaking through the misty, overgrown fields to ambush him and collect the bounty on his head.

"I am certifiable," he muttered, shaking off the disturbing visions. If he hadn't been forced into isolation, maybe his partner, Levi Allen, would still be alive and his former fiancée, Letty Montoya, wouldn't be blaming him for Levi's murder. Not that she hadn't played a part in the mistaken-identity killing by inviting Levi to move in with her as soon as she'd had the opportunity.

Daniel made a face and set his shoulders. All

he could do at the moment was continue to lie low and let his coworkers in the St. Louis Police Department sort out the facts, no matter how frustrated he became. Chief Broderhaven already believed that Daniel was suffering from PTSD after being the victim of a near-fatal kidnapping. If that wasn't bad enough, he'd been put on leave and ordered into hiding after Levi's murder. Okay. So maybe his reasoning wasn't totally logical these days. That didn't mean he'd make an easy target for assassins. Besides, the whole situation might be nothing more than a series of unfortunate coincidences.

"Yeah," Daniel huffed. "Just because you're paranoid doesn't mean that somebody isn't really out to get you."

He glanced at his dwindling stack of firewood, decided to add to it and stepped off the porch. Complete silence suddenly enveloped him. No birds called. No insects chirped.

His pace slowed, his senses keen. His right palm reached for the grip of his sidearm. The holster was empty! He'd been cleaning the .38 when he'd decided to get some fresh Ozark mountain air. *Stupid move. Careless. Foolish.* The best defense available to him was, at that moment, lying in pieces on the kitchen table. A lot of good it would do him there.

But he did have a long-handled ax on the splitting block. Common sense insisted he did not need to be armed every second he spent in such a peaceful, pristine place. His overburdened mind argued otherwise and easily won, just as something tightened around his ankle and stopped his forward momentum.

He dropped like a rock. Caught himself with outstretched arms. Hit the ground rolling and came up next to the slab of log he'd been using as a chopping block. Heart pounding, he grabbed the ax handle.

Daniel peered into the fog. "If you're out there, come on." Shadowy oaks, sycamores and cedars near the old homestead still provided plenty of cover for would-be assailants, as did the fallow, brushy fields. Soon, when some of the trees had shed more leaves, he'd be able to spot interlopers better.

Breathing raggedly, he remained hunched behind the chunk of oak, waiting. Time slowed. He finally grimaced and accepted reality. "Get a grip, man. There's no threat out there. Not even a hungry mosquito." His cramped shoulders began to relax, his heart following. It was a good thing he was still in his early thirties, fit and healthy, because an older man might have had a coronary on the spot.

"The chief was right. I do need a shrink." Only he couldn't go back to the city for treatment. Not yet. Not until his cop buddies figured out who had killed his former partner and if that attack had been due to error, the way Letty had insisted.

Daniel stood and brushed off his jeans. Something glistened near the ground. A wire? That's what had tripped him?

Astounded, he peered at it. If his enemies had gotten close enough to string that wire, why hadn't they attached a bomb to it or kept coming and killed him while he slept?

Brandishing the ax, he braced himself. The air seemed choked with unseen threats, imagined dangers. In his mind he was once again tied hand and foot, lying helpless on a dirty concrete floor, gagged so tightly he could barely breathe, and waiting for his own death at the hands of the criminal gang he'd infiltrated.

He recalled breaking loose and running blindly through the old warehouse on the outskirts of Springfield, finally emerging onto Battlefield Blvd.

Every nerve in his body was screaming, *Run again!* He made a dash for the farmhouse, boots pounding up the porch steps.

Just as he jerked the dilapidated screen door toward himself he heard a bang and a whine. A bullet slammed into his thigh, spinning him around. The force felt like he'd been hit with an armload of baseball bats.

Daniel clambered to his feet and dove through the doorway, scrambling toward the table. Toward the disassembled .38.

All he had to do was stay conscious long enough to put it back together. Judging by the blood pulsing from his wound, that might not be easy.

"How much farther?" EMT Kaitlin North called to the ambulance driver and paramedic, Vince Babcock. He switched off the siren. "It's just up ahead."

"I think I see it." A third member of their crew, Josh Metcalf, was pointing. "The place looks deserted but don't let that fool you. Like I said, Vince and I were sent out here once before. This guy is a real nut case."

"Terrific." Kaitlin kept bracing herself. The narrow, ungraded dirt roads that had brought them into the back country of the Ozarks were so rough her muscles already ached.

Vince parked the ambulance with its rear doors facing the ramshackle house, then reported their arrival to dispatch. Josh grabbed his jump bag and went for the gurney. Kaitlin was right on his heels, her blond ponytail swinging.

A sharp, loud noise stopped everything. Josh put on the brakes so fast Kaitlin crashed into him and almost took them both down. She keyed the mic clipped to her shoulder. "On scene. Shots fired. Repeat, shots fired."

"Copy that," Belinda replied from the station. "You all okay out there?"

"Affirmative."

"Okay. Hold short. Deputies are on the way."

Her partners seemed perfectly willing to wait. Kaitlin would have been, too, if she hadn't spotted so much blood on the porch. Unfortunately, the front door was closed and plywood was nailed over the windows. "I'll check around back," she announced, racing for the side of the house.

Vince was adamant. "No way, rookie. You heard our orders."

She had. But what good was loitering by their ambulance when somebody might be bleeding to death?

"All I'm gonna do is look," she called back.

Rounding the second corner of the small, clapboard building, she was so startled to see someone coming toward her from the opposite side that she faltered, her blue eyes wide, her pulse racing. "Vince! You scared the daylights out of me."

"That was the idea," he said harshly. "What if I'd been a guy with a gun?"

Kaitlin flushed crimson. "Sorry. I never thought of that."

"Yeah, well, I did." He hooked a thumb. "I found a window with a gap at the top of the boards back there. It's too high off the ground for me to see in. Come on. I'll give you a boost."

Following, she managed a wry smile. "How mad at me *are* you? We know the guy inside is armed. We heard him shoot."

"I don't mean for you to stick your head through the hole." He clasped his hands together to make a step for her. "Just take a quick look then back off."

Shaking from excitement as well as trepidation, Kaitlin put her boot in his hands, strained to grasp the top edge of the plywood and pulled herself up. The board creaked and groaned but held. A brief glance told her plenty.

"There's only one person in the room," she reported. "He's down and it looks like he's unconscious. Hold on a sec." Making a fist she rapped on the glass. The victim didn't stir. "Yup. He's out cold. I can't tell if he's breathing."

"You're positive he's alone?"

"In this room, yes. Can't tell about the rest of the house."

She felt herself being lowered and jumped clear. "Let's go."

Vince was saying, "I'll check on the ETA of the police," as Kaitlin powered around the building. She never slowed going up the porch steps. A screen door hung off to the side like the broken wing of a bird. One swift kick with her boot and the front door popped open.

She had enough good sense to fall back until she'd double-checked the scene. That took mere moments. The unconscious, injured man was as rugged-looking as her partners had reported but not a bit frightening or off-putting the way they'd said. Avoiding the red pool staining the bare floor, she dropped to her knees by the victim's head, pushed back the collar of his plaid flannel shirt and felt for a carotid pulse.

Smiling and gulping in breaths, she looked up and proudly announced, "He's alive! We're in time."

Daniel wanted to speak, to warn his erstwhile rescuers that the shooter might still be out there, watching and waiting. His will was strong. His capabilities were not.

Was that a woman's voice? *Letty?* he wondered. *No.* This person sounded empathetic as well as professional. First responders must have understood his jumbled 911 call and found him. Given the remoteness of the homestead and the fact that he'd done his best to shun everyone since he'd arrived there, that was pretty amazing. Only once, after a passing hunter had reported an armed trespasser acting mentally unstable, had anybody from Paradise checked on him. After that mistaken diagnosis was corrected and the medics turned away, Daniel hadn't been bothered again. Until today.

His eyelids refused to rise. Male voices were issuing orders. Somebody was sticking a needle in his arm and taping it down while someone else slit the leg of his jeans to expose the injury site. A stethoscope touched his chest. He felt the leads of a defibrillator being stuck to his skin to record his heartbeats. His mind kept shouting, "Get me out of here!" yet his lips never moved. This felt like the kind of nightmare where you want to scream a warning but are unable to speak, no matter how hard you try.

"I think we should stabilize and transport ASAP," one of the men said. "He's lost a lot of blood in spite of the tourniquet he made with his belt."

Yes! Do it! Take me away from here!

"I don't know. What's the sheriff's ETA?" another asked.

What had happened to the woman? Daniel wondered. She hadn't said a thing since confirming he was alive.

"Finish packing that wound and let's roll. Doctor's orders," the first man said. "The cops are lost somewhere out here and we can't wait for them to find us."

Daniel wished he could cheer. *Tired. So tired.* It was getting hard to make out the conversation going on around him. He felt his body being rolled, moved, lifted. Someone reached into his pocket and tugged on his wallet.

Finally he heard the woman's voice again. "Back off. You're making the bleeding worse."

"Okay," one of the men replied. "We'll let the docs in ER confirm identity."

"From the looks of him he was probably using an alias, anyway," the other man said. "Rookie, get the gurney and let's go."

Kaitlin and the other two worked as a team, securing and loading their patient flawlessly. She followed the gurney and supported the IV bag, then hung it and grabbed a seat as Josh climbed in with her and Vince slammed the doors. The engine revved. Tires spun, then caught. The man on the gurney moaned.

Kaitlin touched his forehead, noted that he was clammy and covered him with a blanket, leaving his leg exposed so she and her partner could monitor the injury.

"You're going to be okay, sir," she said. Her fingers brushed back his thick, dark hair. His lips trembled and parted as if he were trying to talk.

Kaitlin shushed him. "Take it easy. Save your strength. You can tell the doctors everything after we get you to the hospital."

His "No" was faint but unmistakable.

Astonished, she leaned closer and spoke softly. "It will be all right. I promise. My name is Kaitlin. And this is Josh. We'll take good care of you."

Josh tapped her shoulder. "Knock it off."

"Why?"

"Because his pulse is spiking. What you said was apparently not what he wanted to hear."

"I just told him my name."

"No. Before that. I get the feeling our hermit is not fond of hospitals."

"Ah, I see." She gently patted the patient's shoulder. He seemed to be unconscious again but she explained, anyway. "If we don't get you to a medical facility that's equipped to take proper care of you, you'll be in far worse trouble than you already are. So chill, okay? We've given you a little something for the pain and you should feel better soon. You need to trust us. We're the good guys. It says so on our uniforms."

Again his lips parted. Kaitlin leaned as close as possible, allowing for the pitching of the vehicle. Whatever he was trying to say didn't come through.

"Vitals are starting to normalize," Josh reported.

Kaitlin was more than glad; she was thankful. Every shift, every call, began with a fervent prayer for support and wisdom from God. That she'd survived her wild youth was a wonder she didn't take for granted. Making the most of the life that had come after was her deepest desire. It didn't matter that her parents thought she was a failure because she hadn't finished school to become a doctor. She knew she didn't need an MD degree to help people. This job was just as important. Just as fulfilling.

Laying a cool cloth on the patient's forehead she silently prayed for him and blessed him. His arm twitched beneath the blanket. Kaitlin uncovered his hand to check the IV and saw his fingers moving.

She took his hand. He grasped hers as if she were an old friend. If the contact gave him comfort she was fine with it. Truth to tell, something about this patient seemed familiar enough that she, too, was comforted. Losing a patient was the worst part of her profession, by far, and it looked as if this one was going to make it. That alone was such a relief it brought unshed tears.

She averted her gaze to keep Josh from teasing her about being such a softy. Her reputation on the job was pretty good, if you didn't count the scoldings Vince had given her for being too impulsive. The fact that he was right didn't help. She knew she had to get a better grip on her enthusiasm and do things more by the book if she intended to survive her probationary period and be hired as a paramedic when she was fully certified.

The only thing she could not do—would not do—was step back when a life was truly in jeopardy. She might not be a superhero but she was smart enough to know how to act in an emergency. That was a special gift denied to most. When civilians screamed and fell apart, she and those extraordinary people like her kept their cool and did what was necessary. Even as a child she'd been that way. Now that she possessed the right training she felt totally confident and whispered, "Thank You, Jesus."

The hand she was holding tightened on hers. Once again the patient's lips moved. She leaned closer to listen. He wasn't whispering an amen to her prayer. He was saying, "Danger!"

TWO

A trauma team was waiting when they arrived in Paradise and immediately whisked the patient away.

"I'll help you guys finish restocking supplies before I clock out," Kaitlin told her partners. "Dee should be here soon to take over for me."

Vince made a sour face and Josh chuckled at him. "You look like you'd rather have the rookie stick around."

Vince huffed. "Makes no difference to me."

Kaitlin joined in the friendly taunting. "Yeah, right. Sheriff Caruthers's daughter is your favorite teammate."

"I never said that, either."

Josh and Kaitlin both laughed. "No kidding." Her attention was drawn to an arrival in the adjacent parking lot. "Well, well, look who's here." Not only was Dee Caruthers arriving, she was being officially escorted by the sheriff himself.

Kaitlin stripped off her gloves and waved at

her longtime friend. "Hi, Dee. You missed all the excitement."

The brunette twentysomething shot a wary glance at her father. "No problem. A peaceful shift is fine with me."

Kaitlin could hardly hold back her excitement. "Not me. You won't believe the call we just worked."

Rolling her eyes, Dee approached. "Gunshot wound. Dad told me. That's why he came along." When she got closer she lowered her voice and leaned in. "He's been giving me fits again about being in a dangerous job. I keep reminding him I'm not law enforcement the way he is."

Kaitlin grinned. "Does that help?"

"Nope." She peered into the ambulance. "I guess I waited long enough. You got it cleaned up already."

"We did," Kaitlin said, still smiling. She checked the time. "If you don't mind, I'm going to grab my purse and run in to see how our patient is doing." To her chagrin, she felt herself blushing.

Dee picked up on the telltale sign immediately. "Oooh. Is he good-looking?"

"I'm worried about him, that's all. Don't you care when you transport a critical case?"

"Sure. And then I set that aside and move on. You'll have to learn to compartmentalize if you expect to last at this job. You can't get personally involved. It'll drive you crazy."

"I suppose you're right. But he's the first really critical patient I've worked on since I started here. Besides, there's something about him that's a puzzle. I must have seen him before. I just don't know where or when."

"Right." Dee waved Kaitlin off. "Go on. Check on his condition if it will make you feel better. Then go home and get some rest."

"I know I won't be able to sleep until the adrenaline wears off. I can't believe the rush I got. No wonder first responders love their jobs."

"Most of them do," Dee replied with a sigh. "I'm beginning to wonder if it's time for me to get a different one, maybe teaching at a preschool or something safe like that."

Kaitlin shuddered and shook her head. "Not me, thank you. Kids are scary, sticky, ornery and loud."

"What are you going to do when you have your own?"

"I'm not. Ever," Kaitlin vowed. "I know I'd make a lousy parent. I'd probably expect my kids to be doctors or lawyers and stars in their fields, to boot."

"Yeah, sorry." Her friend patted her on the arm. "I forgot what you went through." She brightened. "But look where you ended up. At the top of your

EMT class and already halfway to becoming a paramedic. That's nothing to be ashamed of."

"I know. Thanks." With a sigh Kaitlin started to turn away. "Take it easy tonight."

"Will do." Dee cast a surreptitious glance at the waiting ambulance. "You never told me who your mystery man is. Anybody we know?"

"I don't know him. I suppose we may have passed on the street, although I think I'd have remembered." She blushed. "It should be against the law to look that good when you're bleeding to death."

Dee smothered a chuckle. "Hah! Well, let me know if he turns out to be interesting. You may not be in the market for a husband, but I am."

Amusement at her friend's candid remark stayed with Kaitlin. She located the injured man as they were wheeling him to a room. His leg was bandaged and his pupils were mildly dilated when she checked, meaning he had pain meds on board.

She made small talk with two nurses maneuvering the gurney. "How's he doing?"

"Better than expected," one of them said. "It was a through-and-through. Missed the femur. Came close, though."

"What about a name? Did you get one?"

The other nurse giggled. "Depends on which one you pick. His wallet had two different IDs."

"Really?" Now Kaitlin was really curious. She

eyed the quiescent man. "When I first saw him I thought he looked familiar. What did he actually say?"

"Not much. He sure wasn't happy when I found a police identification card with his picture on it tucked behind his fake driver's license."

"He's a cop?"

"Apparently. Either that or he stole the wallet."

Kaitlin stood back until the other two finished with the patient and left, then reached for his chart and began to read. *Dave Roark?* That didn't ring any bells. *Daniel Ryan?* Kaitlin racked her brain. For some reason *Daniel* sounded right. She stared at his scruffy but appealing face, trying to picture him without the dark stubble. Something was bothering her. She just couldn't put her finger on it.

"What happened to you?" she asked softly.

The patient looked asleep. It not for a flutter of his eyelids she might have thought he was comatose. Hearing was the last sense to go and she knew there was a chance he was picking up her questions even though he didn't or couldn't reply.

Replacing the chart, Kaitlin leaned over him and whispered, "Listen. You're going to make it. We got to you in time but the next time you call an ambulance, we'd appreciate it if you didn't take potshots at us. Understand?"

Did he? Judging by the way his right hand

fisted the blanket covering him she assumed he was at least aware of her presence. "I'm going to leave you now," she said. "Rest. Sleep as much as you can. I'll be back in the morning to check on you. I promise. Daniel."

As she touched his hand in a farewell gesture, his fingers moved the way they had when she'd thanked the Lord during transport. She gave the back of his hand a quick pat and stopped at the foot of the bed to check his toes. Both feet were equally warm, meaning his wounded leg had adequate circulation. Good.

Moisture gathered in her eyes. She smiled. Her first run with a severely injured trauma patient had been a success. All was well in her world. She wished she could say the same for the shooting victim.

Daniel peeked from beneath lowered lids to watch the concerned EMT leave the room. Judging by her questions she didn't remember who he was. But he knew her. How could he forget? He'd broken department rules and received a strict reprimand when he'd allowed her to go home after she'd been caught up in a drug bust involving minors. What he saw now, the useful person Kaitlin had become, proved he'd been right to cut her some slack. Vindication felt good.

He grimaced. Yeah, it felt a lot better than his

leg did. Talk about sore. It throbbed in time with his heartbeats and ached plenty in between despite many painkillers. But he was still alive. This might be an era of fantastic modern medical breakthroughs, but a man could still die in mere minutes from one bullet hole. The fact that the ambulance had found him before he'd bled out, in spite of the leather belt he'd tightened above the wound as a tourniquet, added to his sense of awe. And thankfulness.

"So, now what?" What, indeed? Daniel figured he was in the local hospital in Paradise. The problem was, they knew his real name now. If word got back to St. Louis and his whereabouts became common knowledge before he had a chance to make new arrangements, he was in big trouble.

Testing himself, he raised on one elbow. His vision blurred. His thoughts swam. They had him so doped up it was a wonder he was even conscious. The next time he was offered something to dull the pain he must refuse, he told himself. Hurting was better than dying because he was happy and clueless. If it became necessary for him to try to escape he'd need all his wits about him.

Further movement brought a core-deep groan. He gritted his teeth against the thoughts he couldn't suppress. How far did the influence of the men who had ordered the hit on him spread?

Could they have cohorts in Paradise? Maybe even the sheriff or town cops? It was certainly possible.

He trusted a few special officers in his home department, including the chief, but somebody on the inside had to have revealed his hiding place. Otherwise, the guy who'd punched a hole in his leg would never have located him.

Forcing his eyes to stay open, Daniel stared at the door. Anybody or anything could be on the other side. Watching. Waiting for a chance to finish him off. He knew that.

He also knew there wasn't a thing he could do about it.

Kaitlin phoned the hospital first thing the next morning. Planning a second visit with the man she'd helped rescue gave her an energy boost despite the fact that she'd tossed and turned during the night.

As soon as she was told the patient was awake and alert she donned her uniform to give herself visible authority and started for town. The drive had seemed unending, the hospital corridor miles long. His door was ajar. She rapped, anyway. "May I come in?"

A woman's voice answered. "If you must."

Kaitlin gave the door a push. A lithe, raven-haired beauty stood beside the bed, holding Daniel's hand possessively and eyeing the interloper. "You don't look like a regular nurse."

Kaitlin was grinning. "That's because I'm not. I was on the ambulance that brought the patient in last night." She focused on only him. "How are you feeling today? Better?"

"Yes, thanks. And thanks for saving my life."

"I had help, but you're welcome."

His dark eyes seemed to bore through her. "You don't know who I am do you, Ms. Kaitlin North?"

That took her aback. "How do you know my full name? Did my partners tell you last night?"

"No. I was too busy bleeding to ask."

A smile lifted the corners of his mouth, making her insides tremble. Maybe Dee had been right. Maybe taking a personal interest in patients was foolish. This one was certainly unsettling her.

"The hospital nurses told you about me?" she asked.

"Actually, no." He drew his hand over his newly shaved cheek and continued to smile at her. "Think again. No beard. St. Louis. Five years ago. That park by the arch. Remember a beat cop hardly dry behind the ears?"

"That was *you*?" Tears gathered. She blinked them back. "I don't believe it!"

"Believe it," Daniel said with tenderness, then quipped, "We have to quit meeting like this."

The woman standing beside the bed was scowling. "Care to let me in on the joke, darling?" Bitterness colored her query and she drew their clasped hands to her chest as if declaring ownership, daring Kaitlin to interfere.

Although she had no romantic intentions toward the injured man, his companion's attitude set her on edge.

Apparently, Daniel felt the same because he jerked out of the woman's grasp and avoided her reach when she tried to reconnect. "This is Letty Montoya, Ms. North. She and I were engaged until she decided she preferred my partner over me."

"Oh, dear." Embarrassed, Kaitlin started to withdraw. "So sorry to intrude."

Daniel stopped her. "Don't go. I want to know all about how you put your life back together after I drove you to your parents' place." He looked her up and down. "You obviously got your health back."

"Yes. I did."

"Your mom and dad must have been overjoyed."

"You could put it that way."

"No?" He was frowning.

"Do you remember what I told you that night? Well, they weren't glad enough to have me back to make them change. But I stuck it out. They did pay for rehab and my classes to become an EMT. My prior medical school training made it easy."

Letty huffed with undisguised disgust. "Lovely. Now, if you're done reminiscing, Daniel and I have personal matters to discuss. In private."

Kaitlin shrugged. No way was she going to let herself be thrown out by the likes of that woman. What did Daniel see in her, anyway? Guilt for prejudging a stranger rushed in and convicted Kaitlin before she could think of a snappy retort. The injured man, however, had no such problem.

He pushed himself up and grimaced. "No, Letty. We have nothing to talk about. You made your choice and it wasn't me. You need to leave."

Tears began to cascade, mascara running, as Letty sobbed. "It's all your fault. You owe me."

"I don't owe you a thing," Daniel snapped.

Letty made a grab at him. "Please. I have nobody left, Daniel. You—you have to marry me." Raising her reddened eyes she looked into his stern face. "There's a baby coming."

Kaitlin hoped she hadn't gasped aloud. This was like watching one of Dee's soap operas. It was super embarrassing to see but fascinating at the same time. "I really should go," she said, backing toward the doorway.

"No," Daniel barked. "It's not mine and she knows it."

The weeping waned. "But you love me. You said so. We can get married like you wanted. I'll make you happy, darling. I promise I will."

"Out!" he shouted, pointing to the exit. "Now."

Hands covering her mouth, sobs shaking her shoulders, Letty ran into the hallway.

"Shut the door," he ordered Kaitlin, then added a softer, "please?"

She tried a smile. "Well, since you asked politely…"

"I'm sorry you had to hear that. Letty broke up with me months ago and I thought all the fighting was over."

"She seems sorry now."

"Yeah." He raked his fingers through his wavy dark hair and shook his head. "She didn't get what she'd bargained for."

"The other guy ditched her?"

"No," Daniel said soberly, sadly. "Levi was murdered."

"Whoa! That's terrible."

"Yeah." He rubbed his leg through the blankets as if that would hurry the healing. "The police think the bullet that killed him was meant for me."

Speechless, Kaitlin stared. Daniel's gaze captured hers and held it. The suffering she saw in his expression was unmistakable. There were so many things she wanted to ask that she didn't know where to begin. One fact was evident. He had been using an alias for a good reason.

"You were in hiding here in Paradise?"

"Yes. My chief sent me to that old homestead

in the hopes my department could break up the gang that was out to get me."

"There's really somebody after you? You're sure?"

"Unless this was a hunting accident, the way your sheriff assumes," he said with a gesture at his bandaged thigh. "I'm not done for, so I'm not positive. Hit men usually have better aim."

"Terrific. It's nice to know they take such pride in their work."

Shock was quickly replaced by his laugh. "You're something else, Ms. North. You know that?"

"Call me Kaitlin," she said. "We saved each other's lives. We should be on a first-name basis."

"Agreed."

"So, Daniel, suppose you fill me in?"

"You already know too much. It's better if I don't reveal more."

"Better for who?"

"For you. Letty's coming here is bad enough. She could have been followed."

"What did Sheriff Caruthers say when you told him you'd been attacked?"

"He figured a careless hunter shot me and I didn't argue." Daniel waved a hand as if cleaning a dry-erase board. "I don't trust anybody. Okay? It's not that I think your sheriff is crooked, it's just that I can't be certain who he might talk to."

Scowling, she reminded him, "He knows your real name. It's on the chart. There's a good chance he's already contacted law enforcement because your girlfriend showed up. Where have you been working?"

"Still in St. Louis. I don't have anybody special there but I did have friends. And a partner I trusted until he moved in with Letty and paid the ultimate price." He paused, rubbing his leg and wincing. "That's why I have to get out of here ASAP."

"Impossible. You shouldn't be moved, let alone stand."

"Yeah, well, that can't be helped."

"And here I was thinking you were intelligent. You have no proof your real identity has been shared with the bad guys. That woman, Ms. Montoya, didn't seem like the kind who would purposely out you. After all, you're no good to her and her baby if you're on the root side of the lawn."

"I do not intend to marry her, or anybody else. I should have realized that my job is too dangerous to take the chance of jeopardizing a wife, let alone kids."

Kaitlin was about to agree with him when Letty burst through the door. Her eyes were wild, her face flushed.

She pushed Kaitlin aside and lunged at the bed, grasping Daniel's arm and shaking him. "We have to go. Now. They're here! I saw them."

THREE

It took Kaitlin several seconds longer than Daniel to react, but once she'd made up her mind he saw decisiveness fill her expression.

Grabbing Letty's arm she wrenched it away, insinuating herself between the patient and his ex. "Leave him alone. He shouldn't be moved."

Letty reached out. "He'd better be."

Daniel understood his ex's sense of dread because he shared it. Until they knew who had shot Levi and killed him, anyone could turn out to be the enemy. Kaitlin, however, seemed fearless. That was not a plus. Not in this case.

He managed to slide off the bed and stand on his own. "I can handle myself. Get me my clothes."

"You won't want what you came in wearing," Kaitlin said. "It's a mess. It's also probably been bagged as evidence. You were shot, you know."

"I know the importance of that better than you do," he told her. "These guys mean business. Letty's right. I need to get out of here before they find me and other people get hurt, too."

"And go where?" Kaitlin stood firm, hands fisted on her hips, feet apart in a no-nonsense pose. If Daniel hadn't been filled with dread he might have laughed.

"Scrubs, then. Get me some of those."

When neither woman moved, he shouted, "Scrubs!"

Instead of heading for the door to do his bidding, Kaitlin pointed at Letty. "Go down the hall, third door on the left. That's a linen closet. You know his size better than I do."

Surprised, Daniel scowled. He'd expected the EMT to fetch him something to wear. The fact that Letty obeyed, although reluctantly, was a surprise.

As soon as the door closed behind the other woman, Kaitlin threw her purse onto a chair, dashed to the closet and pulled down a clean, folded, hospital-green outfit. She thrust it at him and turned her back. "Hurry up. It won't take her long to figure out I sent her on a wild-goose chase."

"What? Why?"

"Because of the way she warned you." Kaitlin rolled her eyes. "Think, Daniel. How did she know she was seeing the hit men? How would she know who they are?"

Kaitlin was right. She was a civilian, yet she'd just bested his professional logic. Even if Letty wasn't responsible for the danger he was in, she was clearly not revealing everything she knew. And he had blithely accepted her advice as if she were totally innocent.

Dressing rapidly would have been harder if his adrenaline had not kicked in. He felt like an idiot. How long had he been fooled? And by how many of his former cohorts? There was no telling how much inside information his enemies were receiving.

His guttural "Ready" brought Kaitlin to his side. He looped one arm over her shoulders, figuring she'd help him walk all the way out.

Instead, she guided him to a wheelchair and pointed. "Sit."

"I can make it on my feet."

"Maybe. But if we have to run, I'd rather have wheels under you. Sit, or I'm leaving."

"Okay, okay. You don't have to get testy."

She shot him an incredulous look as she locked the brakes on the chair. "Apparently, I do."

"I'll draw more attention like this than I would if I walked." Nevertheless, he lowered himself and held his leg up while she carefully propped it atop a raised footrest before placing green booties on both his feet.

"Not after I get through with you, you won't,"

she declared. A blanket tucked around him came first, then a towel that draped over his head and covered his hair as well as masking the sides of his face. "Put your head down and pretend you're sleeping."

Daniel did as she asked, marveling at her quick thinking and wondering what other tricks she had up her sleeve. If he had been alone when Letty had arrived with the warning, he might have let himself be led to the slaughter.

He huffed. *Might have?* He would have. That, or the killers would have located his room and taken care of business right there. It didn't matter how it happened, he'd have been finished.

Pulling the blanket close to hide his arms and hands, Daniel kept hold of the leading edge of the towel and braced himself with his good leg, his foot pressing the footrest.

The door swung open with a push from Kaitlin, barely missing his raised leg. He gritted his teeth.

She swung the chair to the right, into a branching hallway. "Where are we going?" he asked.

"What difference does it make?"

"None. Just get me out of here." She knew this hospital, he didn't. Where he'd have wandered, perhaps gotten lost, she was right on track. He hoped.

They passed room after room, most occupied. He had to escape before anybody started shooting. Stray bullets would find plenty of innocent targets in a place like this.

The chair briefly rose on one wheel as Kaitlin spun him around another corner. Daniel gasped.

She slowed and leaned over him from the back. "Sorry. Did I hurt your leg?"

"I'm too worried about your driving to know," he snapped. "Try not to dump me in a heap, okay?"

"You are one ungrateful patient," she replied wryly. "Here I am, rescuing you, and all you can do is complain."

"Are you ever serious?" he bit out, bracing for the next jolt.

"Sure, when I don't feel in control. Trust me. I've got this."

He felt her falter for an instant, then pick up the fast pace. Although he couldn't see her he sensed tension. "What just happened?"

"I got a glimpse of your girlfriend at the far end of that hallway. She wasn't alone."

"Terrific. How many?"

"Two."

"Did they see us?"

"I don't think so. Hang on."

As if he wasn't already. Letting go of the towel, he gripped the armrests of the wheelchair with both hands. Kaitlin was pushing him straight at a bank of closed glass doors! Why didn't they move?

Just as he was about to shout, the doors slid open. Tight passage dislodged the blanket. He made a grab for it.

"Let it go. We're almost in the clear!" she ordered, sounding like a kid on the downward slope of a roller coaster, enjoying every minute of the thrills.

"This is *serious*," Daniel insisted, speaking over his shoulder.

"I know. Do you want me to weep and wail like your girlfriend did or get you out of this mess?"

"Point made." His grumbled reply turned into a series of groans as she bumped his chair off a low curb and started to push him across the paved hospital parking lot. "Are you looking for potholes to hit?"

"Yup. How'm I doin'?"

There was no understanding her, he concluded. The meek, frightened girl he had once rescued had matured into a mix of Nurse Ratched, Wonder Woman and Hot Lips Hoolihan in that old TV series set in the Korean War. If one of her personalities didn't get him hurt or killed, the others might.

He bit his tongue when they bounced through another series of shallow pits in the asphalt surface. Before he could comment again, Kaitlin pushed him behind a pickup truck and stopped so suddenly he almost slipped off the seat.

"Ack!" Daniel righted himself. His forehead was dotted with perspiration despite the cool, autumn weather. Not only was his companion out of breath, so was he.

She rounded the chair and bent over, hands on her knees, gasping for breath and grinning. "We made it."

"Right. Now what? I can't stay here long or they'll figure out where we went."

"I…know. Just…chill."

Daniel wasn't worried enough to keep from feeling contrite. "I'm sorry. I know that had to be hard on you. Are you okay?"

"I will be." Grasping the edge of the truck bed she straightened enough to peek over it. "So far, so good. Nobody followed us."

"What now?"

"We steal a getaway car."

"What?" His gaping jaw snapped shut when he heard her chuckle.

"Relax." Kaitlin grinned. "This is my truck. All I need is the keys and we can take off."

"Where are they?"

"In my purse. In your room."

All the air seemed to go out of him. His shoulders slumped. "My room?"

"Yes, but I know other ways in. Don't try anything funny while I'm gone. I'll be back in a jiffy."

Daniel grabbed her wrist to stop her. "No. It's too dangerous. That room is the first place they'll search and Letty knows what you look like."

"But the other guys don't."

As she was speaking she was reaching behind her neck. When Daniel saw her long, wavy, blond hair fall loose over her shoulders, his heart, which was already racing, made a little extra jump.

"What about your uniform? She'll surely spot that."

"No worries." Kaitlin stripped off the light blue tailored shirt that bore her first name and the ambulance company insignia and handed it to him. Underneath she wore a plain, sleeveless tank top that matched the navy of her plain slacks. Spreading her arms she twirled for him, obviously pleased with herself. "See?"

"Be careful."

"I will. Wait right there." She sobered and eyed him, head tilted. "Promise?"

"I promise. Just hurry."

He watched her for as long as he could, then hunkered down in the chair. Kaitlin had to make it. She had to come back to him in one piece.

Sighing, he closed his eyes, tried to quiet his mind and prayed for exactly that.

* * *

The hospital corridors were fairly crowded since visiting hours had begun. Kaitlin checked her watch. Shift change was coming, too, and the new nurse on duty would surely notice that Daniel was missing and sound an alarm. She didn't have much time left.

What she wanted to do was press her back to the wall and inch down the hall sideways. She didn't, of course. That would definitely draw attention. Instead, she straightened her shoulders, pasted a passable smile on her face and stepped forward boldly. The rubber soles of her work boots on the polished floor kept her passage silent.

One more turn. Five more doors. Her pulse was thudding so loudly she was nearly deaf to sounds around her. She raised her hand and placed her palm on the door to the room Daniel had just vacated. Something stopped her. *Voices? Yes!* A woman was speaking. In seconds, Kaitlin deduced that Letty was on the phone.

"He's gone, I tell you. I'm in his room and the bed's empty." The other woman sounded panicky. "No, I didn't see where he went. He can't have gotten far."

In the hallway, Kaitlin held her breath. *Tell me where they are right now and where they're headed*, she thought, adding, *Please, God*, as an unspoken prayer.

"All right. I'll wait for you here," Letty said, "but hurry."

No! Kaitlin wanted to scream. If she hoped to rescue Daniel from these thugs she had to get to her purse and truck keys. And Letty was in the way. Now what? If she waited until the men arrived there was no way she'd be able to retrieve her purse. Suppose Letty discovered it? Stole it? Kept it? Then what? They'd have no resources that couldn't be traced and little money for traveling.

There was only one thing to do—stage a blitz attack.

Life on the streets as a wild teen had been hazardous and difficult, but it had taught Kaitlin a few tricks. One, an unexpected assault usually worked better than a face-off. The main trouble with a physical confrontation was the conflict with her Christian faith.

"I'll forgive Letty later," Kaitlin vowed. "And ask her to forgive me."

Right here, right now, her task was clear. She had a duty to perform and the tools with which to do it lay inside that hospital room.

Preparing to burst through the door, Kaitlin heard the clicking of Letty's heels on the hard floor. She strained to listen. The sound was receding, then stopped. Could Daniel's ex have spotted her purse? There was no time to waste.

Kaitlin pushed open the door. If it had squeaked Letty would have noticed but it moved on silent hinges. Letty was standing at the window, her back to Kaitlin, concentrating on her cell phone.

Unmoving, Kaitlin waited for just the right second to spring. She didn't want to hurt anybody, not even this deceitful woman, yet she must act boldly and with force or fail Daniel. What good would all her prior efforts do if that happened?

Still facing the window, Letty spoke into her phone. "You won't believe this. I see him! He's…"

Kaitlin rushed her. Knocked the cell phone out of her hand and threw her onto the empty bed.

Letty fought back, kicking and scratching. Her false fingernails raked Kaitlin's bare arms like a hawk's talons as they rolled back and forth, grappling.

The pain actually helped. So did the fact that Kaitlin had been exercising to keep fit for her job. She was stronger, but the spitfire she was trying to subdue was quick.

They rolled to the edge of the bed. Kaitlin grabbed a pillow to try to buffer the blows. That threw Letty farther backward and they slipped off the bed in a tangle. Letty landed first, with a stunning whack to her head.

Kaitlin grabbed the smaller woman's hands and

bound them together with tubing from Daniel's IV. That would do as long as Letty was groggy. There was no time or reason to do more.

Gasping, staggering, Kaitlin lunged for the chair where her purse had been. It was gone! She fell to her knees in despair—and spotted the leather handbag on the floor.

Letty's discarded cell phone lay nearby. Kaitlin could hear a male voice shouting through it. "Stay there. We're on the way."

Rational thought insisted on immediate action despite the fatigue and pain from the fight. Pushing off the seat of the chair with her hands, Kaitlin straightened and grabbed the purse. She ran to the door. Two nurses in the hallway had stopped and were staring at her. That couldn't be helped.

Swiveling, she looked both ways and noted movement to her left. Whoever was headed her way was not wearing white or hospital green. That was enough for her.

Kaitlin went right, clutching her purse to her chest and breaking into a run. She heard a ruckus behind her. Knew the thugs must have discovered Letty.

The final turn was right there. As she whipped around it she chanced a look back. One surly-looking man was at the far end of the corridor, zeroed in on her as if he were a hungry lion and she a helpless gazelle.

Well, she was not about to become anyone's victim. And she certainly wasn't going to let the man who had saved her from the streets be harmed. Not while she had one spark of life left.

Kaitlin plunged her hand into the gaping open top of the purse as she exited the hospital at a run. "Keys! Keys. C'mon, where are the keys?"

Her fingers probed the recesses. She'd switched to a key ring with a furry fob for this very purpose, to be able to locate her elusive keys no matter what. So where were they?

For an instant she wondered if they might have fallen out onto the floor when she and Letty grappled. That notion stuck in her throat like a dry cotton ball until she finally touched something soft and fuzzy. That was it!

Almost to the parked pickup truck she spotted Daniel. Raising her hand with the keys and waving it as if she were leading a cheer at a bowl game, she shouted, "Get in!"

FOUR

Daniel was more than ready. He'd already thought through the moves that would put him in the passenger seat with the least effort or pain and proceeded to execute them. He pulled himself to his feet against the door, looped an arm over the side mirror and balanced on one leg while he reached for the door handle. Gave it a jerk. It didn't budge.

She'd locked the door! An instant swell of anger took him by surprise and he tamped it down. Of course Kaitlin had locked her vehicle. A shift had to be at least eight hours and anybody who knew what she drove would have had that long to steal her truck. If they wanted to.

He almost smiled. Who in the world would take this beater truck when there were so many others to choose from? Nobody, that's who. To say that their erstwhile getaway vehicle was less than perfect was to compare a Ferrari to a rusty bicycle. Still, any port in a storm, as they said.

Momentum took Kaitlin into the tailgate. She

bounced off as if that was the way she always approached. "I thought I told you to get in!"

"Door's locked," Daniel yelled back.

"It just sticks. Give it a yank," she told him as she made her way, gasping for breath, along the edge of the truck bed, then pulled open her own door and threw herself behind the wheel.

Following her directions almost landed Daniel on his back pockets in the lot. Hopping on his good leg he managed to round the gaping door and turn his back to the interior, intending to sit, then push himself up.

Instead, a strong pull on the neck of his scrub top threw him totally off balance. The engine roared to life. He made a grab for the steering wheel and used it for leverage, swinging both legs inside just in time.

Kaitlin's grip was surprisingly strong. "Turn around and hang on. They're coming," she shouted at him. That was all the extra incentive Daniel needed, and a good thing it was, too, because she was already backing out.

Getting the seat belt fastened was difficult but he figured if he wasn't belted in he was liable to break apart from her wild driving. He pulled the strap across his chest and almost succeeded in clicking the buckle in place several times before it finally caught.

That gave him more freedom to brace himself

and try to baby his wound. By this time his leg was throbbing so badly the pain had affected his temper, which had been stretched pretty thin to begin with. "Are you trying to kill us both?"

"Not presently, no."

He saw her knuckles whiten from her grip on the wheel and noted her determined expression. Her chin was raised, her arm muscles flexing, her spine stiff despite the way she was leaning forward, peering ahead.

"Where are we going?"

The instantaneous glance she shot him was incredulous. "You care? After everything we went through to escape you're worried about where I'm taking you? I don't believe it."

Daniel had to admit she had a point. "Not worried. Curious, okay? You aren't planning on turning me over to the police, are you?"

"Because...?" Slowing on the two-lane road as they approached a small town square, Kaitlin peered over at him. "Look at me."

He obliged. "Why?"

"I want you to tell me again that you're one of the good guys. Straight up. Honest. Nothing held back."

Daniel raised his right hand in position for an oath. "I'm one of the good guys. My problem is I can't tell who else is at the moment."

"But you trust me?"

"Obviously."

All he could see was her profile as she turned back to navigating the narrow streets of the town. That was enough. She was definitely smiling. He just hoped that being associated with him never spoiled that smile or brought tears to those amazing blue eyes.

Glancing in the side mirror he checked traffic behind them. It was impossible to tell whether or not his assassins had followed them from the hospital. But one thing he did know for sure. They were out there somewhere. And they would never quit until they were stopped. Or they stopped him.

Adrenaline helped Kaitlin stay on top of things for a while. She could tell it was wearing off when her hands began to tremble and her body felt as though a thief had made off with most of her bones.

The reason she hadn't told Daniel where they were going was simple. She didn't know. If she took him into the hills and hid him there, the way he had been when she'd first encountered him, how could she be certain she wouldn't be making matters worse? Yet, if they stayed around Paradise they were sure to be spotted, particularly if his pursuers had seen her truck leaving the hospital.

That left a bigger city as the only sensible choice, at least for the present. In the Ozarks, a pickup truck was the vehicle of choice for probably half the population. Hiding a tree in a forest had to be easier than making it invisible when it was the only one left standing in a farmer's field.

A quick peek at her passenger confirmed her decision. He wasn't complaining but there was perspiration dotting his forehead, and the muscles of his jaw showed that he was clamping his teeth together, presumably to mask pain.

"Your leg," Kaitlin began. "How is it now?"

"Feels like it has a hole in it. Why?"

"How about the rest of you?"

"Rotten. Just keep driving until I figure out what to do."

"Rest that overworked brain of yours. I already know," she shot back.

The look he gave her in response would have been funnier if he hadn't been suffering. "Who made you sheriff?"

"I got the job by attrition," Kaitlin said. "If you want to take my badge you're going to have to prove you're sound enough to wear it." She reached across and lightly touched his forehead with the backs of her fingers. "Right now I'd say you need sick leave."

"Yeah, well, that's not an option."

"Sure it is." Pulling into a gas station along the way she slipped a credit card from her purse. "I'm going to fill up, get us something to drink and see if they have an ATM. From now on we'll need to use cash."

"TV cop shows again?"

"And street smarts from long ago. You're the one who reminded me of my past. I may as well use what I learned." Pausing at the open window of the driver's door she leaned in. "Anything else you need?"

"Yeah," Daniel said, lifting his hand off his thigh and displaying a fresh crimson blot on the leg of the scrub pants. "I could use more gauze and some aspirin. The stuff they gave me in the hospital is wearing off."

"Not aspirin unless you want to bleed more. I'll find something," she promised. "You stay put."

His cynical chuckle followed her. "Good idea."

As much as she hated to leave him, even for a few minutes, she knew she must plan ahead. Her mental list of necessary supplies kept growing. Above all, the man needed proper medical care whether he liked the idea or not. While he'd been in the hospital his doctors had run antibiotics through his IV. Now that they were on the run she'd have to find an oral substitute.

Done filling her gas tank, Kaitlin pushed through the door to the little store and headed straight for the ATM. Her next stop was the coolers. Cheap foam ice chests were stacked nearby, so she picked up one of those before choosing bottled water, a power drink containing electrolytes and plain orange juice. The more necessities she could charge on her credit card, the better since this was the last time she'd use it.

Not knowing how long their cash would last or how far they might have to go before this nightmare was over left too many open-ended questions. Kaitlin fought off a moment of dizziness and mild nausea. She was hungry. And thirsty. But first things first. Medicine for her patient.

The aisle of painkillers and other over-the-counter remedies offered no bandages other than little sticky strips that would barely do for a skinned knee. Daniel needed more. Better. And there was only one sure way to get proper treatment. She just wasn't sure how she was going to manage that without an attending physician reporting his gunshot wound again. That was the law. He, of all people, would balk at breaking it.

That notion didn't sit well on her conscience, either. In the old days she might have scoffed but no more. Turning her life around had meant a renewed dedication to God as well as the vow to become a stand-up good citizen.

Kaitlin glanced out the front window at her parked truck, her burden weighty. That man was counting on her. She owed him. Plus, she prayed every day for the Lord to show her how to help others, how to fulfill her destiny with honor and grace. Given that heartfelt desire and corresponding prayer, how could she turn her back on anybody in need? She couldn't. She wouldn't.

The problem wasn't whether or not to help Daniel, it was how to best go about it while keeping right and wrong separate. For instance, it was wrong to tell a lie, yet if the truth meant her patient might die, what then? The Bible held lots of examples of lies ruining people's lives but it also spoke of thwarting enemies. That was how she must view this escapade, she reasoned. It was a case of good versus evil and she was on the right side. She had to be. There was no way she'd ever believe that the kindhearted cop who had once granted her a second chance would now deserve the punishment of death.

Paying for her purchases and adding a bag of ice for the flimsy cooler, Kaitlin lugged it all back to the truck and set it down by the passenger door. "How're you doing?"

"I'll live."

"That's the idea." She handed him the sports drink. "Start with this. I have water, too, but you look like you need more."

"I need a cave to hibernate in." He shivered. "And maybe a blanket."

"The last one I gave you, you threw away," she quipped, hoping to lift his spirits.

His "You made me do it" was emphasized by a mock scowl.

"I did, didn't I? They don't have everything on my shopping list at this place. I figured to make one or two more stops."

"Before?"

She sighed, then confessed, "Before I take you to an urgent care clinic for a prescription. You need antibiotics. Badly."

"I can't show up at one of those." Pausing to chug some of the drink, Daniel eased back against the seat, making Kaitlin wonder if he was about to pass out again.

"We'll figure something out," she said. "Trust me."

Judging by the way his dark eyebrows lifted he found her suggestion of trust impossible. Nevertheless, he also seemed to realize he had no choice. He might not have the background in medicine that she did but the man was no fool. He knew he was sick and his fever was spiking. He also knew it was necessary to let her take the lead until he felt better. That would do. She didn't care whether he agreed with her decisions or not. As long as he followed orders that would bring healing she'd be satisfied.

Kaitlin got herself a bottle of water, stowed the ice chest in the bed of the truck and weighted down the lightweight lid before sliding behind the wheel and passing him a small pill bottle. "This is all they had that won't make you bleed more. You can take more than the suggested dose as long as you don't go over four thousand milligrams a day. I'd start with four tablets if I were you."

He washed them down with the remainder of the sports drink. "Thanks. I owe you one."

Despite the dire situation Kaitlin laughed. "Oh, you owe me a lot more than one, mister. And we're just getting started."

Laying his head back with a guttural moan he closed his eyes. "No doctors. Please. I can't chance being put into a computer system that may connect us to the hospital."

"Then what would you suggest? A veterinarian?"

"Only if you know one personally," Daniel said as she pulled out of the gas station heading north.

"Nope. But I did go to school with a nurse practitioner who ended up working in Springfield. I'm hoping she'll agree to see you without reporting a shooting."

"Fat chance."

"Yeah, I know. I'm going to ask, anyway. If she'll treat you and hold off notification of the authorities we'll be okay. All we really need is a good head start."

"And wings. And maybe a gun for me," he countered.

"The wings I can't manage but the gun is a possibility. It can't be a handgun like you had at your hideout because there'll be a waiting period. How about a rifle or shotgun?"

Daniel was scowling when he opened his eyes and turned to stare at her. "Are you serious?"

"Always," she teased, knowing he'd get the subtle joke.

His "Right" was an exaggerated Southern drawl followed by a smirk that she found amusing enough to relieve some of the tension between them.

"Hey, I'm figuring this out as we go along, okay? So far I haven't done that badly."

To Kaitlin's surprise he reached across and touched the back of her hand. Electricity shot up her arm straight to her heart. Any emotional connection she'd sensed in the past had now been proven. She was supposed to be there. Supposed to be helping him. It was as if she were on a divine mission and no way was she going to back down, no matter what.

If, as she believed, God had put the two of them together for the second time, she was duty bound to continue, to do whatever she could, to go wherever their path took them, until Daniel was safe and healed.

Those mental and emotional assurances buoyed her courage and renewed her strength. One way or another, her heavenly Father was going to bring them through this valley of looming danger and show them the mountaintop on the other side.

The analogy was straight out of Christian music, Kaitlin knew. It didn't matter to her. She was more than willing to make use of anything that would carry her along, would give her the extra courage she needed.

"Now I really am worried," her wounded companion said as they halted for a red light.

"Why?"

"Because you're smiling," he said cynically. "You're scary enough when you're driving like there's a T. rex on our tail. Looking pleased about it is terrifying."

"I was never afraid to look under my bed or in the closet," Kaitlin said. "I don't believe in monsters."

"Well, you'd better start believing in human ones." Daniel was rubbing his knee below the bandages. "I've met some."

"Yeah. So have I." Although her smile faded, she managed to keep from frowning. "We'll make it through this," she assured him. "I know we will."

When he didn't answer she noticed he was staring into the outside mirror. "What? Do you see something?"

"Not sure," Daniel said.

Kaitlin could tell by the set of his jaw that he

was uptight again. She saw the chance to make a quick right turn as the light changed and took it. To her relief, the vehicle Daniel had been watching didn't follow. None of them did.

Seeing him start to relax helped raise her mood. "Better?"

"Yeah. For now."

"Then close your eyes and try to get some rest. I'll stick to back roads as much as possible and work my way toward the clinic. It's not too far from that famous sporting goods store."

"Springfield is not my favorite city," he muttered.

"Care to tell me why not?"

"Maybe later," Daniel said. "Right now I'm going to take your advice and try to rest."

"Okay, but don't be too agreeable or I'll worry you've lost your will to fight."

"Only where you're concerned," he replied. "I'm still plenty ready to take on the rest of the world."

No witty comeback occurred to her so she stayed silent. He might think he was ready but she knew better. The fever signaled the beginning, not the end, of his recovery. Without making use of modern medicine he was no better off than a soldier wounded on an ancient battlefield. More of those died from the complications of infection than from their original wounds.

Kaitlin had been observing Daniel as they drove and realized his condition was worsening. Given his obvious intelligence and the fact that he was a cop, he probably knew it, too. That meant she'd have two battles to fight. The one against raging bacteria and the one for his mind.

Once he believed he was done for, it would be doubly hard to pull him back from the brink. The only plus their likely pursuers provided was a continuing threat. Having them in the picture was good for Daniel because it gave him a reason to want to recover and fight again.

Kaitlin huffed, disgusted by the way her brain kept coming up with crazy scenarios. And yet, in retrospect, she had seen it work before. The threat at the hospital had brought out extra strength and conviction. All she had to do was stay far enough ahead of the hired assassins to keep them both alive.

FIVE

Relieved of some of his pain and totally exhausted, Daniel managed to doze on and off for the next half hour or so. Turns and a change in speed woke him. "Where are we?"

She checked the GPS on her cell phone. "Almost to the clinic."

Reality dawned. "I recognize the area. Listen, there's something you need to know."

"Will it help me help you?"

"Maybe." He cleared his throat. "I'm not the most popular guy around here."

"What did you do? Rob a bank?"

"I'm trying to be serious, Kaitlin." He gestured. "Why don't you pull over so we can talk?"

"Okay. I can use a break. Anyplace special?"

"In a crowd would be good. Pick a mall and park in their lot."

"Got it."

Daniel didn't want to tell her about his failure but saw no sensible alternative. Since his capture by and escape from the gang he'd infiltrated while working undercover, most of those criminals were doing time. Still, there was a slim possibility they would accidentally run into somebody who recognized him from his false persona.

Killing the engine, Kaitlin unfastened her seat belt and swiveled to face him. "Okay. Shoot." She blushed and waved her hands as if erasing an invisible chalkboard. "Oops. Bad choice of words. Sorry."

"If you had said, 'Hit me with your best shot,' I'd have been more worried," Daniel told her. "I used to work this part of town. It was an undercover assignment. I actually managed to infiltrate an organization that was distributing drugs and was about to inform my chief when the members of the gang got wind of my true background."

"Oh, no!"

"Oh, yes. They tied me up and beat me before getting into an argument about who was going to have the privilege of putting a bullet in my head." He could tell he had Kaitlin's full attention. He didn't want to frighten her unduly but figured she'd be a lot safer if she were prepared.

"How did you… I mean, you must have escaped, right?"

"Yes. Barely. I worked the ropes loose and waited for a chance to make a break for it. As soon as I thought I'd make it, I ran. Almost got caught."

He held up his hand with thumb and forefinger fractions of an inch apart. "Made it by this much."

"Wow. Is that why you were in hiding?"

"Not entirely." Daniel drew a deep breath before continuing. "Arrests were made and I went back to work in St. Louis, thinking the Springfield job was over."

"I take it it wasn't."

"No. Letty—you met her—decided being married to me was too dangerous, too iffy. In the time I'd been gone she'd fallen for my partner, Levi Allen, and he'd moved in with her. That's what she was talking about in my hospital room."

"I'm sorry."

"Wait. It gets worse. Apparently the guys who'd been sent to kill me weren't too bright because they followed Letty home and shot the wrong cop."

"Now it makes more sense."

"Yeah. She twisted the facts and blamed me for everything. It never seemed to dawn on her that she'd played a part in getting Levi killed."

"But why go into hiding? Wouldn't you have been safer among other cops?"

"If I'd thought I could trust them all, yes," Daniel said. "The problem was, somebody had given the gang an inside tip about who I really was. There weren't many people privy to that information. Letty was one. Levi was another."

"And your chief?"

"Yes, but he's one of the only ones I'm sure is on my side. He had to order me into hiding to get me to go."

That explanation was true as far as he'd taken it. What he hadn't said, and didn't intend to reveal unless absolutely necessary, was that the aftermath of his kidnapping had left him with panic attacks and vivid nightmares. No matter how often he told himself he was stronger than that buried fear he couldn't seem to escape it.

Call it PTS for post-traumatic stress or just plain emotional scarring, he had it. Bad. And he intended to keep his flaws hidden as long as possible, particularly as far as this pretty woman was concerned.

He huffed, imagining her reaction to a full confession. She was liable to drop him at the nearest police station and wash her hands of the whole affair. Then he'd be up the creek with no paddle for sure.

"Look," Daniel said, watching her face for signs of distancing. "I don't want you involved any more than you want to be, but right now I'm out of options. I promise I'll take off on my own just as soon as I'm able to drive."

Instead of answering or arguing, Kaitlin opened her door and started to get out. *Oh, no! Was this it? Was she dumping him?*

"We can cross that bridge when we come to it," she said flatly. "So, water or sports drink for you? I'm thirsty."

That was all? Daniel could hardly believe his eyes and ears. She didn't argue or lecture him or anything. She merely accepted his explanation at face value.

That was almost enough to convince him to tell her everything. Almost. But not quite. If and when he happened to flip out and relive his captivity in her presence he'd have to explain. Until then, it was his secret. Truth to tell, he was kind of ashamed in spite of knowing that that adverse reaction to trauma was one way the brain coped with overload.

Daniel forced a smile as Kaitlin climbed back into the truck toting the entire foam ice chest. She slid it into place on the seat between them.

"I'm thankful this is an old truck," she said, "so it has a bench seat instead of buckets."

"Right." Satisfied that she was through asking questions, Daniel relaxed a little. The throbbing in his leg kept time with his heartbeats and he could tell he had a fever because he felt overheated when the air temperature was moderate if not cool.

"This friend of yours," he began, "is she liable to help?"

"Yes, I think so." She brightened. "Hey! Did they give you back your wallet?"

He shook his head. "I assume it's being held in evidence along with my clothes."

"Do you happen to remember the number of your driver's license? Not the real one, the fake."

"I think so. Why?"

"Because we may need ID at the clinic. All you have to do is tell the truth. You left it behind during the confusion when you were hurt."

"I doubt that excuse will work but you're welcome to try. That devious mind of yours scares me sometimes," he said with a quirky grin.

Kaitlin laughed. "Only sometimes? Huh. I guess I'll have to try harder."

As Daniel watched she sobered and stared into his eyes so deeply he almost shivered. "There is only so far I'll go," she said. "I won't purposely break the law unless it's a life-and-death situation. And I won't harm anyone. Ever. I meant it when I rededicated my life to the Lord. I'm in all the way. Please remember that."

"You're doing the right thing by helping me," he countered. "You know that, don't you?"

"I choose to assume so." She lifted the white foam lid. "So, what'll you have? Your wish is my command."

Daniel wanted to give voice to his fondest wishes for her safety and well-being but he held back. Nothing would be gained by making their situation more personal. As it was, he'd had to stop himself from taking her hand when they had casually touched. If he allowed himself to feel too much, to care too much, to think of Kaitlin as anything more than a friend, he would be doing her a disservice, not to mention making himself crazy. Crazier.

Taking the bottle of cold water she offered, he looked beyond their truck and scanned the busy parking lot. No particular menace stood out. No vehicles seemed familiar. Yet they were out there. Somewhere. And they still intended to take his life to get even.

Nameless, faceless men were waiting for him to make a mistake and Kaitlin's good intentions had carried him right into their neighborhood. Right back into the territory that had nearly cost him his life mere months before.

The more time Kaitlin spent with Daniel and the more she learned, the worse their situation seemed. If he had told her anything about his history in Springfield she never would have brought him here.

And now? Now, he was pretty sick. Taking him farther without getting proper medical treatment could easily be the wrong move. Furthermore, there was the question of what came next. For both of them. As far as she was concerned they were a duo and would remain so until she was given proof that her job was over.

Speaking of jobs, she thought, carefully navigating the busy thoroughfare that bisected the town, hers was probably in jeopardy already. Not only was she skipping classes for her paramedic certification, she could miss her next shift on the ambulance crew.

It took mere moments for her to realize she had her priorities straight. The man beside her had been thrust into her safekeeping as if she was his only real hope. She had to stick with him, to keep helping him. It was the right thing to do.

Signs for businesses in passing strip malls were a jumble of names and colors. If not for her phone's navigation app she would have sailed past the small storefront urgent-care clinic without noticing.

Daniel pushed himself more erect in the seat. "Are we there?"

She waved her phone. "Yes. I've decided to chance telling my friend the whole truth and throwing you on her mercy."

"*You've* decided?"

"Yup. My truck, my rescue, my decision."

A sigh from him became a groan as he tried to move his leg. Lack of further comment worried her more than an argument would have.

She pulled her keys and grabbed her purse.

"Stay here and wait. I'll go find my friend and set things up for you."

All he did was nod and close his eyes. Perspiration glistened on his forehead and dampened the scrub top with patterns of darker green. The worse he got, the more sure Kaitlin was that she had made the right choices.

Passing through the waiting room, she dreaded the likely germ-ridden atmosphere. Considering all the snorting, sneezing and coughing going on around her, she wished she could hold her breath through the entire visit.

A portly, motherly-looking receptionist slid back a glass partition. "May I help you?"

"I'm here to see Mags—I mean Margaret. We went to college together."

The woman picked up a telephone receiver and spoke into it. Kaitlin couldn't hear every word but she got the gist of the conversation. The receptionist doubted her credibility and wasn't shy about saying so.

Nevertheless, a tall, slim nurse practitioner in a white physician's coat came hurrying from the rear, arms open, smile beaming. "Katie! I haven't see you since we both got booted out of med school."

"Those were the days." She accepted Mags's embrace. "We always did want to do things our way."

"Moral code over rules," Margaret said.

"Yes." One arm around her waist, Kaitlin drew her friend aside and spoke privately. "That's the kind of problem I have now."

"Uh-oh. What did you do?"

"Saved a cop's life."

"What's wrong with that?" Mags was fingering the earpieces of the stethoscope looped around the back of her neck.

"Nothing, except he's hurt and can't go to the hospital."

"Why not?"

"It's a long story." Kaitlin cleared her throat and reached for her friend's hand. "We need your help."

"So, bring him in."

"Can't. He needs to stay under the radar to stay alive. It's complicated."

"I imagine it is." Margaret was shaking her head but starting to grin. "What have you gotten involved in now?"

Kaitlin shrugged and matched the other woman's grin. "Oh, nothing much. Just kidnapping, murder, assassins and drug gangs." She would have mentioned Letty, too, but that would have taken too long to explain.

"So, nothing serious."

"Right. Listen, we just need antibiotics and first-aid supplies. I can treat him myself."

"You like prison jumpsuits? Orange will clash

with your blond hair." The nurse practitioner sobered. "I'm sorry, kiddo. I can't prescribe without examining the patient, not even as a favor to you."

"Okay." Kaitlin could identify. "He's out in the car. Can I at least wheel him in the back door?"

"Wheel?"

"Yeah. He's not steady on his feet right now and I'd hate to see him fall and be injured worse."

"Okay. That I will permit." Mags approached the receptionist and leaned over her desk to speak softly, then straightened. "I'll see your friend in a back exam room. There's access off the alley. The door is marked but locked. Drive around. I'll be waiting."

Kaitlin gave Mags a brief, ecstatic hug and almost ran back to her truck. At first she didn't see Daniel. Before she had time to panic she jerked open the door. He'd pushed aside the ice chest and was lying on his side across the seat.

"Are you okay?"

"Keeping out of sight. Did you get the meds?"

"We will. Soon," she told him. "Sit up and scoot over. We have to move around back."

Although he did push himself into the passenger's seat it wasn't without considerable groaning and grimacing. Kaitlin could tell he was also dizzy because he blinked rapidly and steadied himself by grabbing the dash.

"Hang on," she said, trying to keep the worry out of her voice. "It won't be long now."

There was no nod from him, no acknowledgment. He simply held on, his breathing shallow and rapid. This was not good. Not good at all. One plus surfaced to confirm her earlier choice. Coming straight to the clinic had been for the best. Now all she had to do was get her friend to put off immediately reporting a bullet wound and they'd be home free.

She started the truck and backed out. A black SUV slowly cruising up the lane between parking areas captured her attention. Should she mention it to Daniel? See what he thought?

No, Kaitlin told herself. He had enough to worry about. Added strain on his physical resources could push him over the edge and leave her manhandling the body of a muscular six-foot-tall man. She had to protect his last ounces of strength or they'd both be in trouble.

"Lay over the ice chest," she ordered. "It will bring more blood to your brain and keep you out of sight at the same time."

He raised his left arm and used it as a pillow without argument or comment. Kaitlin had been keeping an eye on the suspicious SUV until she'd looked in her mirrors while pulling the rest of the way out. When she looked back, it was gone.

Was that good? Of course it was. Her patient's

paranoia had merely influenced her otherwise sensible thoughts and made her unduly jumpy.

After wheeling around to the rear of the row of single-story buildings she slowed until she'd located the clinic door.

It was opening. Mags was waiting with a wheelchair.

Kaitlin sighed. Everything was going to be all right.

SIX

Daniel was disgusted with himself. If he got much worse he'd pass out cold and he knew it. How much more could he take? And how much more could he ask of his rescuer? She'd already gone far beyond expected. That spoke well of her character.

A tall, no-nonsense woman in a long white coat hustled them into an exam room and shut the door. His slightly blurred vision did not hide her rising temper as she eyed his injured leg.

"What in the…"

"He was in a hospital," Kaitlin explained. "That's where he was first treated. We had to leave in a hurry and I didn't have a chance to pick up fresh bandages or meds."

"Why?"

"Why did we have to leave?" Kaitlin cleared her throat and laid a hand on his shoulder. "It's complicated."

"So you said. That's not good enough, Katie. Spill."

Daniel braced his arms on the wheelchair and tried to hold still as the nurse practitioner slit the leg of the scrub pants. That gave him instant pain relief, meaning his thigh had swollen since he'd dressed.

He made eye contact with Kaitlin and asked her, "Can you cut off both legs so they look like shorts? That way we can get to the bandage and get rid of the stain."

"Smart." She gave him a wan smile as she proceeded to remove the covering on his good leg and trim up the rough edges on the wounded side.

Her friend had withdrawn and was standing aside, arms folded across her chest, scowling. "Well?"

"I don't want to reveal more than I have to," Daniel said. "I really am a cop but I have no way to prove it to you. And there's a hit squad chasing me."

"Looks like you ran too slow." Margaret did not appear convinced.

"They got me when my guard was down," he countered. "After I landed in the hospital they came after me there. If it hadn't been for Kaitlin I'd probably be dead by now."

While he'd been explaining, Kaitlin had gloved up and removed the old bandages.

Daniel gripped his throbbing leg with both

hands, hoping to stop some of the radiating pain, as the nurse bent to assess it.

"The bullet's out?"

"Yeah," Daniel told her. "It was a through-and-through."

"Well, that's one good thing." Margaret was glowering at Kaitlin. "If you hadn't brought him somewhere for treatment it wouldn't matter who was after him. This wound would have done him in."

"That's what I figured."

"And now you expect me to do what?"

He was looking back and forth between the two old friends as though sitting in the stands watching a tennis match.

"Give me supplies, mostly," Kaitlin said. "You know what he needs."

"Probably." Mags handed him a digital thermometer and began to pile bandaging and gauze pads in his lap. "Once you stop hauling him all over Missouri and let him rest, the bleeding should stop. I can't suture it or infection will build up inside."

"What about a broad-spectrum antibiotic?"

Margaret was shaking her head as she focused on him. "Any allergies?"

"Not that I know of."

"What were they giving you in the hospital?"

Unsure, he deferred to Kaitlin. "Do you know?"

"No. I hadn't been planning to make a run for it or I'd have looked."

"All right. I'll give you some physician's samples but I won't write a prescription for a man with no ID. You were never here. Understand?"

Grimacing in pain as Kaitlin began to re-bandage his leg, Daniel nodded. "Thank you."

"Don't thank me. We never met, remember?" Margaret was turning and had placed her hand on the knob when there was a knock so loud the door vibrated. She jumped. "What is it?"

A screeching female voice shouted, "Call the police! We're being attacked."

That was enough for Daniel. He levered himself to his feet and pushed the nurse back to where Kaitlin also stood, jaw agape.

Slowly easing open the door he peered down the long corridor. Several rough-looking men on the lobby side of the interior window were shouting and throwing anything they could get their hands on. One kept demanding access to the exam rooms. Little wonder the waiting-room chairs behind them had emptied. Standing between the thugs and everyone in the back of the clinic was an obviously locked entrance.

As soon as the leader turned aside Daniel said, "Stay here," and slipped into the hallway. Passing three closed doors he peeked inside each room. They were unoccupied. The fourth held an elderly man, thin and stoop-shouldered, keeping his baggy trousers up with suspenders.

"Go out the back," Daniel commanded, his voice raspy.

The man stood as straight as his bent back would allow. "Sonny, the name's Barney, and once a marine, always a marine. Fought in plenty of battles. We never run from a fight."

"These guys will have you for lunch," Daniel warned, ducking into the room to protect them both from discovery.

Eyeing Daniel's bandaged thigh, the senior citizen chortled. "Looks to me like somebody already took a bite out of you." He raised his cane. "Stand aside and let me at 'em."

"Unless you have another cane for me, hand that one over," Daniel ordered, admiring the man's courage but hoping to dissuade him from involvement.

"Nope. You're on your own. This here stick is mine." Swinging it to rest on his shoulder like a rifle, he saluted. "Let's go, sonny, before all the fun's over."

Wondering where Daniel was hiding, Kaitlin stuck close to her friend and followed her down the deserted hallway. Margaret stopped at a cabinet and pulled open a lower drawer. "There. Take what you need. I recommend these." She pointed.

Lacking a sack, Kaitlin began to stuff her pockets.

"Take more," Margaret said. "Space the doses evenly, every four to six hours, and don't miss a dose." She reached into a nearby storage space and produced a disposable hair cover. "Put some samples in this. Then you won't drop them."

"Thanks. But Daniel…"

"First things first. Do you want the meds or not?"

"Yes."

"Okay. Here's where we keep gauze and rolled bandages. Take what you want and go stash everything in your truck. The police will be here soon and you don't want to have to explain." She grimaced. "Neither do I."

Still, Kaitlin was torn. If she left, even for a minute, she wouldn't be there to help Daniel, wherever he was. Rationally, she knew he couldn't be in the waiting room yet or his enemies wouldn't still be demanding access. It was probably only a short time until one of the thugs decided to kick down the locked door. Therefore she'd do as Mags suggested and stash her supplies before trying to find and liberate her patient.

The only actual surprise was that he had gone into hiding. Wait! Maybe he was already outside in the truck, waiting for her. Could he have chosen to leave the nurses to fend for themselves?

Impossible as it seemed, that was exactly how things looked.

Disappointed on one hand and relieved on the other, Kaitlin headed for her truck, yanked open the door. Daniel wasn't there.

She deposited the bulging scrub cap on the floor and emptied her pockets onto the seat, then raced back to find him. To rescue him again if necessary. To spirit him away and save him from infection as well as more physical harm.

The metal door had swung closed behind her! And locked.

With Daniel inside. And she was stuck in the alley.

If he hadn't been hampered by his aching thigh, Daniel could have easily outdistanced his strange new ally. Instead, he and the elderly man approached the melee together.

The receptionist was curled up under her desk, hands over her ears. Daniel paused by a raised counter. Made eye contact with one of the burly thugs.

"Police are on their way," Daniel announced. Although his voice was firm he had to keep one hand on the counter for balance. "Get out of here."

"Hah! Knew it was you." The thug looked over his shoulder. "Told you it was him."

In the half second it took the assailant to raise

his gun, Daniel had ducked out of sight and taken the old man with him.

Shots made the windows vibrate and splintered holes in the interior door. Without knowing exactly what caliber and make the pistol was, Daniel couldn't be positive it was empty. They might never have a better chance for a counterattack, though.

Approaching sirens were enough to convince him to hold his position and wait for law enforcement. The wail was rapidly building. Patrol cars were almost on scene.

He sagged against the nearest wall. The old man passed him the gnarled walking stick. "Guess you need this more than me, after all. Take it, son. I carve 'em outta hickory. Got a dozen more at home just like it."

"Thanks."

"Why're they chasin' you?"

"Long story."

"Figures. I got a few I could tell you, too. I remember once…"

Daniel held up a hand to stop him. "Quiet. Listen."

His heart begged him to be wrong. His mind insisted. Besides screeching tires, wailing sirens and the shouts of fellow officers storming the building, he'd heard another voice. One he knew well by now.

Somehow, Kaitlin North was on the wrong side of the locked interior door. And, true to form, she was screaming orders to the cops and berating the hit men as if they were naughty boys instead of cold-blooded killers.

Adrenaline flooded his body, took over his brain, sharpened his senses and erased pain.

Daniel raised the gnarled cane, jerked open the door and rushed into the fray.

Kaitlin had tried to explain what was going on as soon as the first officers had arrived. Nobody paid the slightest attention to her. Guns drawn, they stormed the clinic with her right on their heels.

Across the waiting room, silhouetted in an open doorway, Daniel Ryan looked every inch a gladiator ready to face hungry lions. She'd never admired him more. He was acting the fool by showing himself but that didn't change her opinion of his courage under fire. When she'd heard those shots she'd feared the worst, yet there he stood.

Ducking and weaving she managed to avoid most of the grappling men in her path. By the time she reached Daniel he was on the floor, on his back, straddled by some civilian trying to strangle him.

A potted plant ended the struggle when the ceramic broke over the attacker's head. Spitting dirt, Daniel pushed him off.

Kaitlin gave him a hand up. "What are you doing out here?"

"Saving you."

She didn't appreciate his gruffness but this was not the time to complain. Instead, she nodded toward the police officers who were quickly gaining control of the situation. "I'm fine, but you could use rescuing." She lowered her voice. "Unless you want them to take you in, too, we need to get out of here."

Although his jaw was rigid and his eyes narrowed, he agreed. "Yeah. Where are you parked?"

"Same place as before. I got locked out and had to run around front to get back in."

She ducked and grabbed his hand, drawing his arm across her shoulders to help him walk. "Let's go."

"Is your friend all right?"

"Yes. And I have the meds we came for."

Sensing his hesitation she gave him a slight push. "Move it. They don't need any more help."

"No. There was an old man… I have to be sure…"

"You mean the guy over there swinging the chair?"

Daniel snorted. "Yeah. Him."

In spite of everything she saw a smile begin

to quirk her patient's lips. It was easy to mirror him, to share the amusement. "Friend of yours?"

"Yeah. As long as Barney is okay we can go."

"Glad to hear it," Kaitlin shot back, half dragging him down the hallway. "I'm getting sick of rescuing you."

He sounded a bit breathless when he countered, "Hey, I was rescuing *you* this time," but she was satisfied just the same. As long as he could think up witty comebacks he wasn't that far gone.

He was, however, plenty heavy. If he hadn't had the cane to also lean on she didn't know if she could have managed to get him all the way to the truck and loaded.

She slid behind the wheel and turned the key. "Hang on."

"When have I ridden with you and not?"

"Very funny."

There was one more thing she wanted to do before hitting the road again. She had to see for herself if the black SUV she'd noticed before was still near the clinic. If it was, they needed to be sure all the assassins had been taken into custody. Leaving just one on the loose could be disastrous.

Daniel leaned forward, his hand braced on the dash. "Where are we going?"

"I want to check the parking lot while you grab a drink out of the cooler and take your first pill.

I thought I spotted a suspicious vehicle when we got here and I want to see if it left."

"What if it didn't?" He swallowed the medication.

"Ask me later." Kaitlin could follow his reasoning. He should be concerned. So was she. But it seemed logical to at least try to find out how many enemies they had and what their vehicle looked like, assuming she'd been right about it.

"Later may be too late," Daniel countered. "This truck doesn't exactly blend in."

"Sure it does. Missouri is filled with old pickups. Half the people who go to my church drive them. Even the pastor does. His is just cleaner than most." She glanced at his bandage. "I'm surprised your leg looks okay. Your blood pressure must have been through the roof when you got in that fight."

"If I hadn't heard your voice I would have stayed out of it," Daniel said.

"You really were coming to save me? Aww."

"Didn't your mother ever teach you it's not nice to make fun of heroes?"

"Not as I recall. She was more into which fork to use or how to throw a perfect garden party."

"At least your parents helped with your education."

"Yes." Concentrating on finding the black SUV, Kaitlin didn't look over at him but she could tell he commiserated. "There. That one, I think. Check out the license plate when I drive by."

"No!"

"What do you mean, no? There's a pencil and paper in my purse if you need to write it down."

"That's not what I meant," Daniel yelled. "There's somebody sitting behind the wheel. If he is who you think he is and he sees us, we're in deep trouble again."

"Rats."

He was glowering at her. Kaitlin could feel the anger coming off him in waves.

It was too late to back up and if she stopped suddenly and blocked the aisle that would call more attention to them, so she maintained her speed until they were past.

Finally, she chanced a peek at her passenger. "Well? What did you think?"

Daniel was hunkered down in the seat and peering into the side mirror. "I think you'd better get out of town," he grumbled. "That black SUV is backing out of its parking place."

"Coincidence?" She looked for herself. He was right. And they were blocked by police cars stopped at all angles in front of the clinic, their emergency lights still flashing.

Hands clamped tight to the steering wheel, Kaitlin managed to slip between the rear bumper of a parked car and the side of one of the patrol units.

Excitement had kept her from remembering to pray beforehand but success deserved a whispered "Thank You, God" when she was in the clear.

"I don't know how you did that."

"Neither do I." She gave a nervous laugh. "I was holding my breath."

Daniel's loud "Ha!" made her jump.

"What?"

"He tried to follow us and hit the cop car."

"Oooh, that's gonna leave a mark."

"I sure hope so."

It was a relief to hear his mood lightening. Kaitlin checked behind them once more and saw the other driver backing up. He might not have made it through the narrow passage she'd used but he was far from stuck. As soon as he could reverse far enough down that aisle he'd be after them again.

She merged into traffic and scooted to the far left lane, putting as many cars between them and their pursuer as possible.

"Can you see him?" she asked Daniel.

"Not yet. But if he is after us he won't be far behind."

"Yeah. I figured." Facing front and leaning forward as if that would make the truck go faster, she made a face. "Sorry about that one. I was wrong."

Blurting another sharp "Ha!" he added, "It's

almost worth all the trouble we're in just to hear you admit a mistake."

"It could still be a coincidence."

"You really believe that?"

She shook her head. Her jaw clenched. "No. Not for a second."

SEVEN

"We need more supplies," Daniel said flatly. "If you stop someplace after we leave all this traffic we'll be too easy to spot."

"What are you suggesting?"

"That world-famous sporting goods store. You know the one I mean. It's not far and they have acres of parking. It'll be easier to get lost in the crowd there."

"And we do need a gun. At least you do. I've never even touched one."

"Another lapse on your parents' part. Even if you never fire a shot you should be taught gun safety."

"There are pros and cons."

"About use, yes. Safety is another thing. Nobody can guarantee a person won't be thrust into a situation that will require knowledge of firearms. It's basic, like knowing when to cross the street and when to stay on the curb."

"I've got that one down pat, thanks. I don't even know what kind of gun to ask for."

"We'll need something easy to operate. Like a shotgun. I'm not suggesting you go hunting. I just want you to be able to defend yourself if I can't do it."

He knew he was ill. Only God knew how bad it would get before the antibiotics kicked in. Kaitlin might not like the idea of going on the offensive but she should at least be prepared to stand her ground. If arming her was what it took, then so be it.

"I'm not real familiar with Springfield," she said. "Punch in the store name on my phone and get directions."

"We won't need to. I know this town, remember?"

Observing the shift in her expression he decided to fill in a little more detail. "My undercover assignment didn't start here. I'm on a task force out of St. Louis. At least, I was. Clues led me southwest and I ended up here. That's when the job went sour."

"The guys you were with figured out who you really were?"

"Yes. And they weren't happy about it."

"I can imagine." Although she didn't turn and look at him he could tell she sympathized by the jut of her chin and the way she pressed her lips together. *Imagine?* She couldn't possibly put herself in his place. Not in a million years.

Thoughts of the panic he'd felt, the conclusion he'd come to that his life was over, hit him so strongly his body reacted as if it were still happening. His gut clenched. His tongue tasted of bile. Every muscle tightened, ready for a nonexistent battle. Only this wasn't the same as what the old marine had meant when he'd talked about combat. This was debilitating.

And totally ridiculous, Daniel insisted to himself, fighting his senses. They were lying to him. He knew what was real and what wasn't, didn't he? Of course he did. The times he had to rally himself and crawl back to reality through the blackness of his mind were getting fewer. Farther apart.

He thought about the temporary home he'd made in the isolated house outside Paradise. Those days had done a lot to settle him, to help him gather his thoughts and control unexpected panic. He laid a hand over his bandage. Until now.

Kaitlin's voice broke into his disturbing reverie. "I said, which way on Sunshine?"

Blinking, he forced concentration. "Um, left. I think. I wasn't paying attention."

"Well, you'd better start," she said crossly. "I'm not positive but I think we have company behind us again."

* * *

Choosing to turn in the middle of the block, Kaitlin took evasive action by pulling into a parking lot and exiting on a side street. Daniel wasn't the only one whose alertness had waned. Fatigue was overtaking her, too, and making her less observant. Knowing how bad that was and countering her weariness were two different things. She'd been on the move since her early shift on the ambulance and the day's events had worn her to a frazzle. Too bad their troubles were far from over.

"If we were rich we could trade in my truck for a different one," she said. "Or if we were crooks we could just steal one."

"You should have asked your friend if you could borrow her wheels."

"Oh, no. We took enough advantage of Mags by going there. I wasn't about to involve her any more than necessary."

Pausing the conversation while she turned again, and relieved to see no other vehicles copying the zig-zagging pattern, Kaitlin frowned over at him. "I hope she doesn't get in trouble for helping us."

"She won't. I'll see to it. Somehow."

Kaitlin could visualize possible scenarios, most of them bad. If they kept running they were bound to make a fatal mistake eventually. Yet what choice did they have? Thinking about his job she pulled out her phone and tried to hand it to him. "Call your boss and tell him now."

"You mean before somebody catches up to us and shoots me again?"

"I wouldn't put it that way," she argued. "I'm trying to work out a sensible way to end this chase." *And I'd be devastated if anything happened to you*, she added to herself. That was the truth, like it or not. In the short time she and Daniel Ryan had been together she felt they had bonded. At least, she had. Every time he winced she felt his pain. Other patients she had cared for had brought out her sympathy, of course, but this man was different. Threats to his well-being sent shivers along her spine and made her tremble, head to toe.

Kaitlin slowed to enter the driveway of a house sporting a For Sale sign.

"What are you doing?"

"I need to rest a minute." She began shaking and rubbing her hands to bring back circulation. "And we need to make a shopping list. I'm too antsy to remember everything I'm supposed to buy when we stop to shop. And I'll need details about the shotgun you want. I'm assuming you won't be going in the store with me."

"No."

She reached for her purse and handed him a pen

and paper, then stretched her shoulders and rotated her head, trying to release the tension.

"We need to pool our resources so we don't run out of money."

She huffed. "You mean you want to know how much I have, right? Last I heard your wallet was back at the hospital or in evidence."

"True." He looked so disheartened it made her ache.

"Hey, don't worry about it. You can pay me back when all this is over. Let's see, I had grocery money before I went to the ATM and I took out the max." She did a quick estimate in her head and cited the total. It didn't improve his mood.

"Okay, forget the gun. It's too expensive. We need other things more, like camping supplies."

"And shoes for you," Kaitlin said. "You can't go tromping around in hospital booties."

"You think?"

"Well, they do match your shorts, but those are pretty messy, too. Put down your sizes and I'll see what I can do."

"Get the cheapest things they have," Daniel warned, "or we'll be broke before we know it."

"There may be another ATM inside."

"Don't chance it."

"Why not? They already know where we are."

"One faction does," he said soberly. "I wish I

could be sure those guys are the only ones after the bounty."

"Bounty?"

"Yeah." He nodded. "When I told you there were guys after me I meant lots of them, not just the gang I was involved with. They put a price on my head. I'm worth more dead than alive."

She blinked rapidly as he took her hand, holding it fast between both of his. "It'll be okay. We'll get through this. And as soon as I'm back on my feet I'd like to take you out for dinner."

Kaitlin hoped he was half as enthused about spending time together as she was. What they needed was quality time when they weren't forced into close proximity for their mutual benefit. What would it be like to relax and just get acquainted without having to keep looking over their shoulders?

To her surprise, that wasn't merely a random thought. She really wanted to find out.

A nagging little voice in Daniel's head kept insisting he had no right to invite any woman into his life in any capacity. Not until he'd stopped having the flashbacks and panic attacks that had caused his chief to place him on extended leave in the first place. So far he had been able to mask his symptoms around Kaitlin, but the cause remained, ready to emerge without warning, rendering him useless at best and perhaps dangerous at worst.

"Hey," he said, forcing a smile when he thought he saw hesitancy on her part. "It's just dinner. I figure I owe you."

Kaitlin rolled her eyes and said, "It better be a doozy of a meal if you expect it to make up for all of this."

"You haven't been bored, have you?"

"Noooo. I can't say I have."

"There. You see? I know how to show a girl a good time."

She huffed. "And you accused me of having a warped sense of humor."

"You do. We both do. I told you before, it's a coping mechanism for cops and firefighters and other first responders. We may not seem normal to civilians but we're run-of-the-mill to folks in our kinds of stressful jobs."

"Agreed."

The way she was studying him was a little unsettling to say the least. He scowled. "What? Why are you looking at me that way?"

"Truth?"

"Always."

"I'm worried about you. About us. Sometimes you act as if you don't take any of this seriously. That scares me almost as much as the gang that's been coming after us."

When she paused he considered volunteering more information. The problem was, he didn't know how much was fact and how much supposition.

Finally, when Kaitlin said, "Tell me more? Please? I feel like I'm tilting at windmills like Don Quixote."

"Interesting analogy," Daniel said. "Look, I'm only guessing about some things. We pretty much decided Letty has to be in on it because she was able to recognize the killers and pretend to warn me. Other than that, I really don't have names and faces for all my enemies. It's my suspicion that others in the St. Louis underworld have it in for me. Maybe a few cops do, too. I just can't be sure. That's the problem. If the good guys wore white hats the way heroes used to in old Western movies it would be a lot easier to tell them from the killers."

"No gang colors?"

He shook his head. "No. These guys are too smart for that. They dress and act just like everybody else so they don't stand out in a crowd. The only way to ID them is to get to know each man. And woman, like Letty."

"She didn't give you any clues about her loyalties before?"

"You mean while I was engaged to her?" Daniel knew there was rancor in his tone but he couldn't help it. "No. Either she's a very good actress or she changed sides after Levi was murdered. I tend to lean toward the latter. What I don't understand is why she was so angry. She's the one who dumped me for him and set him up by letting him move in with her."

Kaitlin was slowly shaking her head and staring, glassy-eyed, through the windshield at nothing in particular. He hated himself for failing to give her the assurances she'd sought. Revealing his emotional scars wasn't going to help, he insisted. If he'd felt strong enough he'd have told her to point her truck northeast and deliver him back to his chief. Maybe that was what he should do, anyway, sick or well. It would get him off Kaitlin's hands.

"All right," he said with a poignant sigh. "Drive me up to St. Louis. I'll be able to recruit other help once we get there."

She rolled her eyes and made a face at him. "Oh, sure. And hope you make it alive? It would go over great with your police chief boss if you died of sepsis on the way. Or if we were ambushed before we got there."

"That is a concern."

"Well, duh." She reached for the key and started the engine. "How far to the store you want me to use?"

"Two or three blocks. It fronts on Sunshine.

Prices would be lower at one of those common box stores scattered all over the state, but we'll be able to lose a tail better by sticking to the largest crowd. They don't get any bigger or busier than this specialty sportsman's complex."

He knew he was right. And, thankfully, Kaitlin wasn't arguing. He supposed he should be glad she simply accepted his decision but he remained unsettled. Perhaps that was because he was sending her out alone instead of figuring out some way to go with her. To protect her.

Daniel placed his hand lightly over the bandage on his leg and noticed the skin around it was hot. That wasn't a good sign. Not good at all. Heat indicated infection. The severity of the pain hadn't changed much, but his thigh hadn't been burning up earlier. Despite taking medication he was getting sicker, losing his battle with whatever germs had taken up residence in his leg and were starting to throw a party there, with him as their unwilling host.

Telling Kaitlin was a must. However, the timing of that particular confession needed to be handled properly. If she thought he was actually that ill she might drag him to another hospital. As long as he remained conscious, fine, but if he passed out there was no telling what's she'd decide to do.

"Right at the traffic light," Daniel said, pointing. "That'll take you past the main entrance. That's the one you want."

"Gotcha."

It struck Daniel that she was the most capable woman he'd ever had the pleasure to meet. Considering her rough start and the way she'd turned from the temptations of drugs and alcohol to become a good citizen was truly amazing. The more he thought about wanting to keep her in his life, the more he was convinced how unfair that would be. Not to him, to her.

His thoughts were so intrusive, so disquieting, he barely noticed when Kaitlin pulled into a parking lot and chose a spot. There was no reason for him to micromanage her choices. They were as good or better than his would have been, which didn't mesh well with his pride.

"All right. I'll travel light," she said, stuffing cash and the keys into her pockets. "Give me the list. I'll be back as soon as I can."

He'd been afraid she'd order him to stay in the truck but she didn't say a word about it. Constant pain was making him edgy, and above all he didn't want to lose his temper. They'd been almost strangers when her ambulance had picked him up, yet she'd offered aid when he'd needed it, asking nothing in return. How many other people, men or women, would have been so willing to put themselves out like that? He couldn't think of a single one.

Keeping an eye on her until she'd joined the crowd entering the enormous sportsman's complex, he finally gave himself permission to lay his head back and close his eyes, meaning the respite to last only seconds.

That was the last thing he remembered.

EIGHT

More than a little awed, Kaitlin stopped just inside the entrance of the rustic-themed behemoth of a store and stared. She'd heard about this place, of course, but hadn't imagined its scope and grandeur. Or that so many shoppers would gather under the vaulted ceilings to gawk. No wonder it was billed as Missouri's number one tourist attraction!

Signage pointed out various departments, true, but she could tell that locating everything on Daniel's list was going to require a monumental effort. Not to mention a whole lot of walking.

"Maybe they sell roller skates and I can cut down on how long this takes me," she muttered to herself. So many people. So much noise. Children seemed the most excited about the live fish swimming below a footbridge over an indoor pond. A few of the younger ones had gone into hysterics when they'd seen the lifelike taxidermy of bears, lions and deer, and were being comforted by their parents. According to descriptions she'd heard, there was also a world-class aquarium inside the store somewhere, as well as some kind of wild-life center. The impressive display at the entrance was just to whet visitors' appetites.

Speaking of which, Kaitlin's stomach was growling. Passing an aisle display of energy bars she scooped up several boxes. No telling when they'd have a chance to stop for food. Her patient needed good nutrition as well as antibiotics and hydration. They had drinks in that flimsy ice chest but no decent food on board.

Once her mind caught hold of the idea of actually camping out instead of looking for an out-of-the-way motel she had a better idea of what to buy to keep him comfortable while he fought the fever. If she'd had more cash in hand she'd have gone for high-end supplies. Since she didn't, she improvised with reflective covers that held in heat and a wool blanket instead of a sleeping bag, a rudimentary cooking set and freeze-dried meals.

Finding and choosing Daniel's clothing was next. Shoes in his size were limited to expensive hiking boots, at least in the section she'd wandered to, so she picked up sandals for him in case she didn't find anything else suitable.

Kaitlin knew she was nearly at her self-imposed monetary limit. She pushed her shopping cart out of the way and mentally totaled up what she was about to spend. After she topped off her gas tank they'd be nearly broke.

She huffed and made a face. So what else was new? She'd been out of money before and had survived. She'd do it again. Daniel came first.

Thoughts of him brought empathy. Concern. And a renewed sense that she was being watched. In a store the size of this one it was extremely unlikely she would be noticed, she reasoned, hoping to calm herself.

The display next to where she stood held relatively inexpensive T-shirts with the store logo on them. Kaitlin lifted the closest extra-large one and held it up as if checking the printing while she turned slowly and peered past it to scan the crowd.

Fine hairs at the nape of her neck prickled. She shivered. "Get a grip," she told herself. "You're imagining things."

She had to be. Didn't she? After all, she was an innocent bystander, not anybody's target. At least she didn't *think* Daniel's troubles had rubbed off on her.

What if they had? She dropped the first shirt into her shopping cart, picked up a second and turned to check the aisles behind her. Nothing looked off or threatening, so why were her hands shaking and her knees so weak all of a sudden?

"Low blood sugar," she mumbled to herself,

dropping the second shirt atop the first. "I'm getting out of here."

That, however, was easier said than done. Although dozens of registers were open she still encountered long lines. Having to stand still and wait put her at a distinct disadvantage.

Inching forward, she wished she could somehow become invisible. The longer she stood there, the more uncomfortable she got. "Naturally I chose the slowest line."

A friendly woman behind her laughed. "You and me both. My kids are going to have my poor husband fit to be tied by the time I get out of here." She gave Kaitlin a broad grin. "Do you have children?"

"No way."

"Oh, I thought maybe your family was going camping."

"I just like to be prepared," Kaitlin alibied. "You know, in case of a disaster."

"Have a couple of kids and you won't have to wait for disaster to happen," the woman quipped. "They'll bring it right to you. Still, there's nothing like a family."

Kaitlin had to smile. "I don't plan to have any children."

"Yeah, well, that's what I used to say." The woman laughed again. "Then I fell in love with a guy who was crazy about kids and here I am."

"I'm sure you're a great mom."

"I do my best. My mee-maw used to tell me that was all the good Lord expected."

The line moved forward, Kaitlin with it. She always gave her utmost to any task so maybe she wouldn't be that bad at being a mother. Yeah, right. She could model her behavior after that of her stuffy, overly controlling parents and turn out a child who was so afraid of making a mistake she'd turn to rough street kids for approval. That seemed to be the pattern of her life, didn't it?

Ah, but meeting Daniel back then had helped turn her around, she reminded herself. Thoughts of his kindness warmed her heart and made her smile in spite of continuing uneasiness.

So, so ready for a pleasant daydream, Kaitlin let her mind relax as she stepped up to the check-out counter. She'd forgotten to figure in the sales tax and her bill was higher than she'd imagined, but a two-for-one sale on the shirts that she hadn't noticed helped balance out the error.

She pushed the brimming cart toward the exit. That was when she finally did spot someone staring at her. He didn't look at all familiar, yet there was an aura about him that gave her the creeps. He was leaning back, arms folded, one foot propped behind him against a narrow section of unadorned wall.

If she hadn't looked into the stranger's eyes she

might have overlooked him. Unfortunately, she not only met his gaze, she read it as predatory.

He might be another kind of criminal, she reasoned. Maybe he was simply looking for an easy mark. A woman alone. Someone he could follow to the parking lot and rob. Well, she wasn't carrying a purse and most of the cash in her pocket had been spent, so if he intended to rob her he was going to be sadly disappointed.

Kaitlin shook her mind loose from its inane ramblings and forced herself to focus on the rest of her surroundings. The guy against the wall wasn't the only shifty character present. The notion that she was being stalked made many people look menacing. She'd just about pegged another dangerous criminal when a cute little girl and young woman ran up to him and gave him joyful hugs.

Seeing that made Kaitlin question everything. Had she grown so paranoid that she was seeing enemies where there were none? Apparently. A parting glance at the guy leaning against the wall was fruitless. He was gone.

"I'm being ridiculous," she insisted to herself, having little trouble accepting that criticism. The main door slid open automatically. Kaitlin moved through with a group of other shoppers and made straight for her truck. Whether her senses were right or wrong, she needed to rejoin her patient and get him out of town ASAP.

* * *

Having napped enough to renew some of his strength, Daniel had been shocked to spot a familiar face in the parking lot crowd. Was this the answer to his prayer for Kaitlin's safety? It seemed so. Patrolman Anthony Grainger and he had gone through police academy together. They weren't best buddies but he had no reason to distrust a man he hadn't seen for years.

Careful not to jostle his sore leg, Daniel had climbed out of the truck and, using the handmade cane, hobbled over to where Grainger stood.

"Hey, Tony. What brings you here?"

Grainger beamed as if meeting a well-liked old friend and stuck out his hand. Daniel saw the man's smile fade when he noticed his bandage. "What did you do? Was that line of duty?"

"No. Just an accident. So, are you working in a department down here now?"

"Not exactly." Tony averted his eyes as he explained. "I'm private security these days. Didn't cut it on the force."

"Hey, I'm sorry," Daniel said, meaning it. What a waste of talent. The Tony he remembered had been a top-notch cop.

"It is what it is."

"You can say that again." Although he took pains to appear nonchalant on the outside, Daniel remained alert to possible threats. His initial

idea had been to ask Tony for a ride but he was
rethinking that. How likely was it that somebody
he'd trained with would be loitering here at this
particular time? The sportsman's store was popular, sure, but it made far more sense that someone
who had known Daniel in the past had tipped off
Tony and sent him there.

"So, no uniform? Are you off duty?" Daniel
asked.

"Yeah. Waiting for my girlfriend."

"Ah. Me, too."

Grainger chuckled. "Good to hear. I'd worry
if I thought you were behind the wheel with a
bum leg." His laugh had started to sound nervous.
"Don't suppose it'd be easy to work the clutch,
huh?"

That comment raised Daniel's hackles. Ninety-
nine percent of contemporary vehicles had automatic transmissions, so why had Tony mentioned
the difficulties of pushing in a clutch? He had to
know what kind of truck he and Kaitlin were traveling in. That was the only explanation.

Therefore, Daniel reasoned with building dread,
Anthony Grainger had to be part of his problem,
not the prayed-for solution.

And, in his haste to relieve Kaitlin of responsibility and safeguard her, he had approached the
wrong man.

Now what? If he tried to walk away would

his former buddy grab him? The other man was strong and healthy. It wouldn't be a fair fight if they did tangle. Plus, he had to somehow keep Kaitlin out of it.

Daniel's breathing sped, his heart keeping pace and then some. Kaitlin. She was late. Suppose they had her already!

Nothing looked or felt amiss once Kaitlin was out in the sunshine of the early evening. No wonder she was hungry. The sun was going down and she hadn't eaten a thing since breakfast.

Parked vehicles surrounding her old truck had changed since she'd left it but none was a black SUV. Nor did she see anything like that nearby.

Glad she'd tied the handles of the plastic sacks as she'd checked out, Kaitlin tossed them over the tailgate. The passenger window was rolled down. She expected to see Daniel napping or at least lying down on the seat.

Her singsong "I'm back" was intended to rouse him pleasantly.

Freezing, she did a double take and blinked, trying to wrap her mind around what she was seeing. Or, rather, not seeing.

The truck was empty!

She whirled, ready for a fight that didn't come. A calm, surrounding atmosphere contradicted her feelings. Did she dare shout for him? If he was actually okay, broadcasting his name at the top of her lungs would be idiotic. So was standing there like a lost urchin and waiting for his return.

Quick checks down nearby rows were fruitless. Considering the vastness of the parking areas there was no way she'd be able to cover them adequately on foot. Yet if she moved her truck and Daniel came back he'd think she'd abandoned him. She wasn't merely stuck between a rock and a hard place, she was suspended between a bottomless abyss and the unknown of an astronomical black hole. There was no right answer. There was no correct reaction. No matter what she did it could be 100 percent wrong.

Sliding behind the wheel she backed out, praying as she drove. "Father, keep him safe. Please. And guide me. I don't have a clue what to do now." Following that with thanks and praise for expected answers she laid out a mental grid that would cover that section of the lot while repeatedly bringing her past the place they'd been parked so she wouldn't miss seeing Daniel if he did happen to show up.

That was all she could do.

"Please, Jesus, let it be enough."

While Daniel pondered his next move he noticed Grainger's attention diverting to something in the distance and used the cane for balance as he swiveled to see what.

To his disappointment it wasn't Kaitlin. To his surprise and disgust, however, Tony was looking at Letty. And she seemed to be in quite a hurry to join them.

The other man's hand was in his pocket, leading Daniel to suspect he was armed. At that range it wouldn't have mattered if Kaitlin had gotten him a shotgun, he'd be at a disadvantage due to their close proximity.

"You should have taken her up on the offer of marriage," Tony said gruffly. "We could have avoided a lot of unpleasantness that way."

"What are you talking about?"

"Money, of course. Letty had it all figured out. As soon as you were married she'd be eligible to draw your pension and I could turn you in for the reward."

"You mean kill me and hand me over, don't you?"

Grainger shrugged. "Whatever it takes."

"You're not going to shoot me here in front of all these witnesses, are you?"

"I will if I have to."

Daniel understood perfectly. They were going to kidnap him, haul him into the country and then murder him out there. Too bad it was such a good plan.

At the thought of his prior kidnapping he began to feel his palms growing clammy, his forehead damp. Tremors sang along his nerve endings and twisted his gut in knots. He clenched his fists, fighting to retain control. The only mental image that gave him strength was that of Kaitlin, so he latched onto it and imagined everything about her, the silkiness of her hair, the grace and tenderness of her fingers as she'd bandaged his leg, the stubborn set of her jaw when she was asserting herself.

In his peripheral vision he caught a slight movement. Tony had taken hold of the gun in his pocket and was pointing it at him through the cloth of his windbreaker. As soon as Letty reached them he was going to be outnumbered. Perhaps if he could take this prospective kidnapper by surprise and wrest the gun away he'd have a chance. Was it even possible?

Daniel decided to play the invalid as a distraction. Moaning, he leaned heavily on the cane, almost overacting and actually losing his balance. "Agh. I can't take this pain. You have to let me sit down."

"Soon." The man gestured. "Start walking."

"Wh-where?" Daniel bent over the cane, hugging his stomach with his free arm. "I'm sick, man."

"You'll be a lot sicker if you don't do as I say." Tony called out, "Go get the car."

Letty stopped and cupped a hand to her ear.

"I said, bring the car." This time, Daniel was ready. Straightening as fast as he could, he swung his free arm in a wide arc, connecting with his adversary's nose.

Anthony staggered back. Drew the gun just in time for his arm to become the perfect target for Daniel's cane. The forward thrust and contact did its job but it also pushed Daniel off balance. He staggered, swinging a second time on his way down.

The gun went flying. Grainger leaped. Landed on top of Daniel and drove a knee into the bandaged leg.

Daniel cried out. Grabbed for the man's collar. Drove his own forehead into his enemy's nose and heard a satisfying crack. He had to end this fast or they'd draw a crowd and endanger innocent civilians.

Letty had joined the melee. She was holding Tony's gun and trying to aim, her hands shaking so badly that Daniel figured she was just as liable to shoot her own foot as she was him.

Grainger was cupping his broken nose and cursing, but at least he'd gotten up and was no longer kneeling on Daniel's wound.

Daniel gritted his teeth and got to his knees, using the cane to rise fully. Dizzy and in agony, he knew better than to try to run. Even in his best shape he couldn't have outrun a bullet.

Letty tried to pass the gun to her cohort but he ignored her. Blood was seeping between his fingers and he was caterwauling like a wild boar with its leg caught in the jaws of a trap.

This was Daniel's best opportunity. He had to act no matter what. With lightning speed he slapped a hand against the side of the pistol and made a grab for it.

Letty screamed. The gun fired. Most bystanders shouted and ducked but, as always, there were a few who simply froze, incredulous.

Daniel almost lost his balance again. At the last second he recovered, flipped the pistol around and tried to hold it steady. It wasn't until he had some semblance of control over the situation that he realized he couldn't convincingly explain his actions to the police without telling everybody who he was and increasing the danger even more. He didn't dare stick around long enough for cops to arrive because that was likely to land him in jail. Once in a cell and unable to flee or defend himself, he'd be a sitting duck, the same way he'd been in the hospital.

He began to slowly back away, still holding the gun. Voices in the crowd rose to object, to order him to stop. The action of those citizens would have been appropriate, even welcome, had he been in uniform and able to prove his innocence. As a ragtag, wounded combatant, however, he naturally looked far guiltier than Grainger or Letty.

If somebody did work up the courage to try to grab and restrain him, there would be nothing he could do. They didn't know it, of course, but he'd never aim at an innocent party, let alone shoot.

Not even if his future hung in the balance. Which it clearly did.

NINE

The first clue Kaitlin had to where Daniel might have gone was a small gathering of people and a minor traffic jam. She stopped because the lane was blocked.

A young woman pushing a child in a shopping cart hurried past and Kaitlin leaned out the window. "What's going on?"

"Some crazy guy with a gun," the mother shouted back. "Don't go that way."

"How do you…" But the woman was already too far past to pay heed. Kaitlin stopped the next person hurrying by. "Wait. What's going on over there?"

"Don't know much," an older man said. "Some bum got the drop on a nice-looking couple. I'm not hangin' around to see what he does next."

She asked, "What did he look like?" too late. The witness was already on the run.

Cars ahead were pulling aside wherever they could and clearing the aisle rather than passing the conflict. Kaitlin had no such qualms. She eased forward until the scene was clearer. Bystanders were falling back yet remaining focused on the center of the group. Dark, tousled hair was just barely visible above the heads of the others.

It was Daniel. Without a doubt. What had he gotten himself into now?

Seconds later the crowd had dispersed enough for her to see the answer. He did have something in his hand, presumably a gun, and he was pointing it at some people. That was crazy. He hadn't seemed irrational before and she didn't think his fever was high enough to produce delusions. Not yet, anyway. So what was going on?

More frightened onlookers fell back, either edging away or turning and fleeing, shouting warnings as they ran. This was bad. Really bad.

Although a few intrepid young people were holding cell phones aloft and shooting video, Kaitlin doubted that would be enough to prove Daniel was innocent. Why he had left the truck in the first place was no longer her main concern. Now she wanted to know why he had felt it necessary to face down his enemies.

The dark haired woman must be Letty, Kaitlin reasoned. Otherwise Daniel wouldn't be holding her and another man at gunpoint. So where had he gotten a pistol? Could he have taken it from the couple he was facing? That was the only conclusion that made sense.

As she watched, several fairly young men in the background began to circle, maneuvering to get behind Daniel. He had nowhere to go. No fallback position. Either they or the police would soon have him captured and their fight for survival would end. Badly. She could not let that happen. But how could she possibly help without making the situation worse?

Foot on the gas, she revved the motor. A gray cloud of exhaust billowed behind the truck.

Daniel apparently heard the unusual noise because he chanced a quick glance, disturbing his aim enough to move the muzzle of the pistol to the side.

Kaitlin saw one of his prisoners start to lunge toward him. She let up on the clutch. Tires spun. Squealed. The odor of burning rubber filled the air.

Her truck shot forward as those who feared they might be in her path dove for cover. Everyone scattered except the two Daniel had been accosting.

Hands holding the wheel in a death grip, Kaitlin skidded to a stop directly beside her new friend. "Get in the back!"

They were out of time and options. If he tried to limp around to the passenger door the mob was sure to grab him. Instead, he did exactly what she had hoped.

Hooking one arm over the side of the truck bed he swing his good leg high. Carried by momentum he threw himself over the edge of the bed, landing with a thud and a shout of pain.

Kaitlin didn't wait to see if he was all right. She floored the accelerator, spun her wheels again and turned toward the street. Toward freedom.

"Please, God, let him be okay," she prayed, frantic yet still in control enough to handle the speeding vehicle. If no one gave chase they just might make it.

When she looked in the rearview mirror and saw Daniel waving at her from directly behind the driver's seat, her relief was so intense her eyes misted.

The best part about seeing his hand was realizing that he was motioning her to keep going. Okay, she would.

But when they finally stopped to let him climb back into the passenger's seat, she was going to give him a piece of her mind. Getting out and trying to walk, let alone take on a mob, was probably one of the dumbest things she could imagine. What had he been thinking?

Traffic slowed as police cars approached, sirens screaming, lights flashing, heading toward the sporting goods store. It was going to take them several minutes, at least, before they sorted out the whole story. Even if one of the photo-takers had a picture of her truck and license number it'd be a while before the details were clear. That was to their benefit.

"He's made me a fugitive, too," she muttered to herself, wondering if she'd made a terrible mistake. Logic told her she had. Her heart disagreed. If she believed Daniel was the innocent party, and she did, then she'd had no choice. He'd needed her help and she'd given it freely. Period.

Now it was time to expand on his rudimentary plan and get them out of the city. In one piece. Without being arrested. And without being spotted by those involved in the criminal conspiracy that had gotten them into so much trouble already.

The irony of their situation was almost strong enough to be funny, Kaitlin thought with a grimace. As if they didn't have enough trouble already, they'd now have half the people in Springfield aware of their presence, not to mention that the local news was likely to be picked up in St. Louis, as well.

That was where she was eventually going to have to take him. But right now, right here, he needed rest and continued medical treatment. And to provide that, she had to find a way to become invisible, keep him warm and hydrated, administer meds at precise intervals and change the dressing on his wound to keep it sterile.

Oh, and successfully keep dodging illegal bounty hunters who wanted him dead. This time she permitted herself a weak, lopsided smile. What a mess.

Picturing Daniel, however, her mood lifted enough to warm her heart. To straighten and strengthen her grin. To give her the peace and assurance she had done the right things so far. Unimaginable circumstances had thrown them together and kept them there. Could that be an accident? Kaitlin doubted it. She'd experienced other unexplainable situations and had seen them through, learning later that her prayers had been answered after all, just not the way she had envisioned.

Encountering Daniel Ryan, a man to whom she owed an enormous debt, might be another case of divine intervention. Viewing it as such was certainly comforting.

She glanced in the rearview mirror again. She could see his bare feet and ankles near the tailgate. He wasn't moving.

She signaled for a turn, pulled onto a shady side street and took the chance of stopping in front of a house when she didn't see anyone in the grassy yard.

Leaving the truck idling, Kaitlin slid out, calling his name. "Daniel?"

Afraid she was going to find him suffering more, she was delighted to see his eyes open and blinking at her when he complained, "About time."

That attitude was such a relief she had to give as good as she got. "Picky, picky, picky. Some people are never satisfied."

"Are you planning to let me ride up front now?"

"After the stunt you pulled back there I should make you stay where you are," Kaitlin quipped.

As he raised on an elbow, then pushed himself to a sitting position, Daniel's expression hardened, his eyes glittering with what she judged to be anger.

"I had my reasons."

"They'd better be good ones."

"They are," he replied. "Lower the tailgate, will you? I'm not up to vaulting out the way I got in."

"That was pretty impressive," she told him.

"I had plenty of incentive."

He was still grimacing as he settled himself in the front seat. "My enemies apparently have a lot more friends than I do."

Kaitlin wanted to remind him that he had her, no matter what, but she figured he already knew that. His seat belt was fastened by the time she was ready to drive again.

"There are campgrounds north and east of here," he said. "Did you get everything on the list?"

"All but boots for you. Too expensive. But I did pick up sandals on sale now that summer's over."

"Fine." He laid his head back, his left palm resting on his bandage. "Let's go."

"What happened back there?" Curiosity insisted she ask.

"I made another mistake," Daniel said. "I trusted the wrong person and nearly paid the ultimate price."

"Is that where you got the gun?"

He nodded slightly. "Yeah. If I'd known Letty was with Tony I'd never have approached him."

"Her again?" Kaitlin rolled her eyes. "I didn't recognize her."

"She showed up after I got out to talk to an old buddy from the academy. Looks like my enemies have recruited folks I used to call friends."

"How will we tell them apart? I mean, after we get you back to St. Louis?"

She saw the muscles in Daniel's jaw clench before he closed his eyes and said, "That's the problem. We won't be able to."

Although Kaitlin had stopped and awakened him to take another pill, Daniel kept feeling worse. His fever came and went, accompanied by pain and swelling in his leg. Skin redness had widened beyond the edges of the bandages, further indicating the seriousness of his condition. Every bump in the road sent lightning bolts of pain shooting through him. His head was pounding. And at present, he was so cold he shivered.

"You don't look so good," Kaitlin remarked.

"Really?" His teeth chattered. "I feel wonderful."

Noting the truck slowing, he pushed himself higher in the seat. "What's wrong?"

"I'm going to get you a blanket out of the back."

"I'm fine. Keep driving."

"There hasn't been any sign we were followed," she argued. "I'm getting the blanket. It'll only take a second. And I want something to eat. You should eat, too."

"Did you bring a nice, medium-well steak dinner?" In truth he had no appetite but he wanted to keep up their semi-normal banter so she wouldn't worry more.

"Not exactly. I do have freeze-dried meals. We can cook those as soon as we camp."

"And in the meantime?"

"Trail mix and protein bars. Easy to eat and full of vitamins."

"That's not food. It's hardly an appetizer."

"It'll have to do." She cast him a disparaging look. "You're awfully fussy for a guy whose well-being depends on me."

The truth of that comment set him back. He nodded and reached for her hand. Slim fingers wove between his and he had to admit her touch felt reassuring. "I know. I'm sorry if you didn't realize I was teasing," he said softly. "If I let myself dwell on the fix I'm in it'll…" He stopped himself before he said too much. Before he embarrassed himself. Yes, his emotional problem was more common than most laymen thought. And, yes, he had been through real torture. But as far as he was concerned, that wasn't an excuse. He should have been stronger. He should be now. Yet he wasn't, was he? And that failure ate at him like a ravenous beast.

Feeling Kaitlin's grip tighten on his hand he shook off his self-criticism and forced a smile. "My dad was a cop. Did I ever tell you that?"

"I don't remember hearing it before. Is he retired?"

"He was, until he accidentally interrupted a robbery at a convenience store and tried to stop it all by himself." Hoping she'd get the idea without a detailed retelling, Daniel was relieved to see her nod.

"I'm sorry."

"Yeah, me, too."

"What about your mom?"

"She's adjusting, I guess." And ranting about her foolish decision to marry a cop in the first place. "She has a lot of friends in the retirement community in Florida where she lives. They take trips together, throw parties for homeless people, make quilts for nursing homes. You know."

"Not really," Kaitlin said. "My parents travel, too, but their altruism is confined to writing checks to charities occasionally. I'm not saying that's wrong, it's just so distanced from the actual needs."

Daniel smiled at her. "I'm glad you're not like that, even though you did fund this adventure we're on. I'll pay you back, you know. I promise."

"Then I'd better keep you alive so I can collect," she said, returning his grin.

"That's the idea."

When she pulled her hand away, opened the door and stepped out he was disappointed but had to admit her timing was perfect. Treating their association as if they were on a lark was best for both of them.

Kaitlin returned and chose snacks from a plastic shopping bag while Daniel unwrapped the blanket. A few minutes of holding her hand had made him forget how chilled he was and how ill he felt. Now that their special moment had passed he was more than aware of his rising fever.

The thought of food almost turned his stomach when she offered him an energy bar. "No. Thanks."

"You should eat," she said.

"Haven't you heard the old saying, feed a cold and starve a fever?"

"This is no head cold we're dealing with," Kaitlin reminded him. "This is a lot more serious."

"So is sitting here parked where anybody driving by can check us out," Daniel countered. He'd put the cooler on the floor between his feet. He bent and lifted the lid. "I will drink something. What can I get you?"

"A get out of jail free card?"

"Sorry. Fresh out of those," he said with a telling sigh.

"That's okay," she said, smiling gently. "I'll take a bottle of water instead."

Daniel was so touched by her empathy he had to look away to hide his raw emotions. If he were in the market for a permanent relationship with any woman he'd certainly put Kaitlin North at the top of his list.

Remembering his mother's angry raving after his father's needless, untimely death, he steeled his nerve. Marriage was out. An extraordinary woman like Kaitlin deserved no less than total commitment and a promise of forever. Therefore, he reasoned, he should pray for the right man to come along to make her happy.

That concept was almost ludicrous. If he wasn't good enough for her, who would be? Certainly not any of his cop buddies, assuming he had any friends left on the force. Maybe a doctor? A paramedic?

Each idea made him sadder. Each vision of her as the wife of another man brought deeper despair. To his astonishment, he hated picturing Kaitlin as anyone's wife. Except maybe his own.

"Impossible," he whispered.

"What is?"

"Life," Daniel snapped back. "Just plain life."

Surprisingly, she laughed. "Are you just now figuring that out? I thought you were a lot smarter."

He had to chuckle. "I used to think so, too, until a gang of crooks put a price on my head."

Eyebrows arching she said, "Yeah, there is that."

TEN

Kaitlin could tell her patient was losing his fight against the infection. He could insist over and over that he was fine, but one look at his feverish face told a different story. His eyes had been closed for the last thirty minutes or so. She hoped he was dozing. He needed rest almost as much as they needed to find a place to hole up before dark.

Camping? Her? Except for the experience of living with a group of wild kids in her teens she had zero experience roughing it. Well, so what? She could read directions on the packages to prepare their meals, and until Daniel grew hungry she figured to exist on trail mix and protein bars. She'd done it before. And providing she was careful to limit her own consumption of their supplies, she figured they'd have enough to last a week or more.

And then what? Kaitlin asked herself. Possibilities kept popping into her head, each more dire than the one before, and the weather only served to accentuate her dilemma. Gathering clouds had cloaked what little daylight remained, she had no idea where they were because the GPS on her phone insisted they were off the charted grid and the supplies she'd bought did not include anything waterproof—except maybe the silvered blanket-like covers she'd added to save money.

At the first hint of rain she was going to have to bring all their gear out of the back of the truck and cram it into the cab with them, so she decided to pull off the road and do it right away. If she didn't find proper shelter soon they were going to have to spend the whole night that way.

Nothing about this situation was funny, though Kaitlin did wish it were. Whoever had cast her as the heroine in this current drama had apparently failed to realize she was not a born country girl. Her instinct for survival might be strong but her preparation for this particular trial was nil.

A flash of lightning made her gasp. Immediately penitent she glanced at the sky. "Oops. Sorry, Father. I don't mean to complain but could You show me where to go? Where to turn? Where to hide?"

Daniel stirred. Opening his eyes he peered into the dusk while he rubbed his neck. "Why did we stop? Where are we?"

"I was just asking God the same question."

"Seriously?"

"Yes and no. GPS is out. I could use some guidance."

"I have an idea where we are," he said. "I'm just surprised you drove way up here."

"Up where?"

"Lake of the Ozarks. See that sign?"

A weathered billboard advertising a defunct fisherman's resort stood halfway between the road and encroaching forest. Kaitlin nodded. "Do you think that place is still standing?"

"Parts of it are," he said.

Noting the tension in his body and the way his jaw muscles were clenching, she was more than wary. "You're sure?"

"Yeah. Last I heard it was abandoned but I knew some of the guys who hung out there from time to time."

"I take it this wasn't a police department retreat we're talking about."

"No. It was a hideout for anybody who wanted to dodge the law." He pointed. "Drive on. I'll tell you where to turn. The road we want is just around the next bend."

"How far from there on? I was going to bring the rest of our gear in so it stayed dry."

"It's not raining yet. Keep going. We're safer there than we are out in the open like this."

Although she followed his orders she did so with keen misgivings. Once they were off the two-lane paved road and away from what little traffic there was, Kaitlin stopped her truck again. "I'm going to need a lot more information before I go driving into an armed camp."

"I've only been here once," he told her. "I imagine they quit using the place after they figured out who I was. I assume they thought I'd identified it to law enforcement and it was no longer safe."

"Are they that smart?"

"Some of them are," Daniel countered, wincing as he shifted position and moved his injured leg. "The point is, we need temporary shelter and I know where we can find it."

"What do we do if somebody else is already there?"

"Depends who it is." He grimaced. "All I know is we can't go on like this. You'll give out and I'm already useless. It's worth taking the chance."

Kaitlin pushed in the clutch and dropped the old truck into low gear. When she accelerated this time the engine growled like an angry bear about to go on a rampage.

"Well, they'll hear us coming for sure," Daniel said. He rolled his eyes.

Picking on her was one thing. Disparaging her beloved old truck was another. "You can always get out and walk."

"I'll ride, thanks."

"Thought so."

"Sorry."

"For what?"

He huffed, causing her to glance his way. "For being critical when I know you're doing all you can to get us out of trouble."

That was better. "Apology accepted. Will this trail take us all the way or should I be looking for more signs?"

"This entrance is a straight shot, but it's pretty rough. If your four-wheel drive works you may want to use it."

Instead of responding directly, Kaitlin reached up and engaged all four wheels, then patted the dashboard. "It's okay, baby. He didn't mean it. You're doing a great job."

"You talk to your truck?" She could hear a muted chuckle in his tone.

"If course. We're buds. And if you don't stop picking on her she might just quit." It was amusing to watch him puzzling out her comments and deciding whether or not she was serious. Finally, she said, "Relax. She loves me. She'll keep going in spite of your rotten attitude."

"Good to know."

"Speaking of knowing," Kaitlin began, "what can I expect at this so-called resort?"

"A roof over your head, if nothing has changed for the worse. I know it won't have improved." He shifted, grimaced and continued. "The cabins and most of the lodge are uninhabitable by anything except wild animals and insects. The main room, however, had a working fireplace and fairly decent furniture the time I was here. You can build us a fire and we'll be warm enough."

Kaitlin didn't like the task he'd picked for her. "It's not that cold out."

Daniel shivered beneath the blanket he'd pulled around himself. "Feels like it to me."

Right. His fever. Of course he'd need added warmth. She'd provide whatever he needed, even if it meant swallowing her pride and asking him how to build the fire. It couldn't be that hard.

"What about the smoke? Won't it be noticeable?"

Leaning slightly to look up at the sky he shook his head. "Not on a miserable night like this one promises to be."

"Sounds like an answer to prayer to me," Kaitlin said, smiling. "I wanted a good hiding place and here we are."

"Wait till you see the lodge before you get too thankful," Daniel said, sounding gruff. "It's a dump."

"A safe dump?"

"Relatively."

"Then I'm still thankful." It was easy to tell his pain was increasing, partly because he had no smart-aleck retort and partly because his jaw muscles clenched against each jolt the truck took from the uneven terrain.

Further thought about the abandoned lodge was reassuring. Even if the roof leaked in a few places, the coming rain was a blessing. It would mask their warming fire as well as wash away any tire tracks they might have left.

Of course it would also cause them to leave behind ruts when they drove away. Ruts that could be followed as far as the highway. After that they could disappear again.

Her hands tightened on the wheel. *Unless they've guessed where we're going and are waiting for us on the paved road when we try to leave.*

It had been Daniel's goal to describe the lodge as worse than it really was so Kaitlin wouldn't be shocked when she saw it. As their headlights swept across the front of the building he realized he'd fallen short. It was far more dilapidated than he'd remembered. The only thing good about that was stronger assurance it was no longer in use, even temporarily.

"Nice," Kaitlin drawled with more than a hint of sarcasm.

"So is your truck."

"Touché." She was shaking her head slowly as the headlights illuminated the collapsing porch. "I think my truck comes out on top in this contest."

"Yeah. If I remember right there's a rear entrance. It should be safer than trying to go in this way."

"And nobody will spot my beautiful truck."

"Right." To his disgust, large rain drops were beginning to dot the windshield. "Better hurry."

"Ya think?"

"All right, all right. I don't mean to boss you. It's just what I'm used to doing at work. A hard habit to break."

"I'll keep reminding you until you get over it."

"Thanks loads." A particularly hard jar made him grab for his leg through the blanket and yell.

"I did not do that on purpose," Kaitlin insisted. "Can't see the ditches under all these leaves."

Breathing hard and trying to keep from making any more involuntary outbursts, Daniel said, "That one sneaked up on me, too. Pull up next to the door over there so we can get the supplies inside before they're soaked."

"I'm going to let that order pass," she said, "because I was wondering where it was best to park."

He faced away from her to roll his eyes. The qualities of courage and intelligence that he so admired about Kaitlin were the very ones that set them at odds. Too bad he couldn't have it both ways, wasn't it?

Recalling how she had driven straight at the gun-wielding ex-cop in the parking lot gave Daniel more shivers. Kaitlin wasn't merely brave; she was crazy brave. That trait had been helpful so far but it wasn't something he wanted to see continue. He'd saved her once and she'd returned the favor. At that point they'd been even. Now, the score was getting unbalanced and he didn't like feeling beholden to her or anybody else.

Opening the door he swung his feet out. The soles of his new sandals touched the ground. He let his weight down slowly, hoping the pain would allow him to hobble at least as well as he had during the altercation in Springfield.

Knives of agony twisted in his nerves and throbbed up his leg into his spine. It was almost severe enough to stop him, but not quite. Pushing through, Daniel rested a moment against the side of the truck, then started for the truck bed where Kaitlin was already grabbing the handles of plastic bags.

"I'll get these. See if the door's unlocked."

"Now who's giving orders?"

"I am," she told him flatly. "If you want to stand out here arguing we're both going to get wet."

Daniel figured his leg wouldn't be good for many trips up the steps to the threshold and into the lodge so he countered. "I'll grab the blanket and the cooler out of the cab while you bring that stuff."

Thankfully, she didn't snap at him this time.

If the pain hadn't clouded his thinking he would have automatically entered first to check the premises, particularly since he still had Grainger's gun. Forgetting his police training could get them both killed, he reminded himself. That wouldn't do. Kaitlin could nurse him when he needed it but he was the cop. The protector. He owed it to her to remain as alert as his condition permitted.

That was the problem, Daniel reasoned as he hoisted himself up into the lodge, pushing the cooler ahead on the dusty floor once it was through the door. He was sick and getting sicker.

The next time he had to confront one or more of his enemies he might not be strong or aware enough to win.

And then what would happen to Kaitlin?

For the first time in memory, he realized with a start, he had thought only of her welfare. Of her safety. Of her future. He had to make sure she survived, even if the price to pay was his own life.

Kaitlin was appalled. The lodge was more than messy and dirty. It was a dump. Nevertheless, she was determined to hide her feelings and, considering how worn out her patient was, that shouldn't be difficult.

The first thing she did was hand Daniel one of the new T-shirts and commandeer his scrub top as a dust rag. One sofa was covered with fake leather.

It was also placed in front of the hearth. She wiped down a place for Daniel and pointed. "Sit."

"You forgot *stay*."

"That was implied," she countered. "I'll see what I can do about finding firewood before it gets soaked." Although she had no experience with tin roofs, the noise was enough to convince her the rain was coming down with such fury it might already be too late to bring in dry wood.

"There should be a dry stack on the porch. Just watch yourself. It looks less sturdy than I remember."

This whole place looks ready to fall down around us, Kaitlin thought. "Right. How much do I need to bring in?"

"Five or six split logs and kindling." Frowning, he studied her. "You've never built a fire, have you?"

"I've seen it done. Can't be that hard."

"It is unless you want to burn up all your wood in a hurry and run out," Daniel told her.

"Okay, okay. This time I'll let you show me what to do."

"Smart lady."

"So you've said. I do wish my skill set included more practice in things like this." *Because I may have to handle everything by myself pretty soon*. "How are you feeling? It's about time for another pill."

"I figured." He leaned his head against the leathery back of the couch and sighed. "Go get the wood and I'll tell you how to build a good fire. Then we can look for my meds."

Kaitlin opted to reverse priorities. In seconds she was handing him a tablet and bottle of water. "I may have to go back to town for more to drink," she said, thinking out loud.

"Check the cabinets first. I imagine they drank all the liquor but there may be canned juice or something left."

"Okay. Six pieces of split logs, coming up."

It struck her as she headed for the ramshackle porch that they were in deep trouble. She'd do her best, of course, but Daniel should be in a hospital. And she should be at work on the ambulance crew, studying for her paramedic exams in her spare time. Instead, they were hiding from a hit squad miles and miles from adequate emergency services. Kaitlin shivered. Should Daniel take a turn for the worse his very life could hang in the balance.

She didn't want that responsibility. Not even a little bit.

Fighting to remain conscious and alert, Daniel counted the minutes until he could watch Kaitlin construct the base for the fire and get it going. It was more than a matter of comfort for him, it was necessary if he hoped to recover quickly. Being chilled might feel right with a fever but it was contraindicated. Kaitlin had to know that from her own training.

Any other woman thrust into this situation might have panicked or wept in despair. Not Kaitlin. She was made of sterner stuff and it occurred to him, not for the first time, that her sojourn on the street might have toughened her up to face this very trial. Anything was possible, particularly if a person relied on a heavenly Father and trusted Him in all things.

Doing that had been more difficult for Daniel after his earthly father's untimely demise, yet the hours he'd been held captive as an undercover cop had helped turn him around. Without the faith, the ability to call out to God for strength, he knew he'd have given up. And that would have surely led to his death at the hands of some of the same men who were pursuing him now.

This time, his physical strength was compromised. But he had a partner. A brave cohort who had not only rescued him once, she kept doing it. Unspoken prayers of thanks and pleas for her continued safety raced through his mind so rapidly they were little more than flashes of insight.

That was enough. Daniel knew in his heart that God had heard and would act. His greatest hope was that the divine answer would mirror his fond requests. He wasn't trying to order God around the way he had Kaitlin, he insisted to himself. He was humbly begging that the One they worshipped would have mercy on them and let them go on living.

The concept of living led him straight to an image of the two of them as a permanent couple. Despite the ridiculousness of such a thing, Daniel had to admit the notion had some merit. If any woman had the courage to become a cop's wife, it was Kaitlin, providing she cared for him enough to consider him more than her patient. When he was well, assuming he did recover, he might break down and ask her out on a date. They had teased about it before and she hadn't exactly turned him down.

Fighting sleep in spite of the pain, Daniel chided himself for planning anything in the future. Without divine intervention, he wouldn't be alive then.

ELEVEN

Kaitlin was growing more and more concerned about Daniel. Surely the antibiotics would have helped him by now. She'd made certain he got each dose on time. And he'd been drinking water, although he had lost a lot of hydration via perspiration.

The fire in the hearth had settled into an orange-red glow and she'd dutifully added sections of split logs just the way he had instructed. The fire must not go out until they were ready to move on, she'd told herself, managing to awake from dozing in time to keep the room warm.

Daniel was stretched out on the couch, his head pillowed on an armrest, the blanket tucked tightly around him, while she leaned back in a wooden rocker she'd dragged in from the porch when she'd gone after a second load of wood.

When he awoke he'd certainly be better, Kaitlin assured herself. Perspiration signaled a break in his fever. Mags had included a digital thermometer but it had apparently gotten lost when she'd pitched their supplies into the truck so she could only guess. Touching his damp forehead was out of the question for several reasons. One, it would wake him. And, two, she knew she would enjoy stroking his brow too much. There was an instinct to soothe with touch that she hadn't realized she possessed until now. Until Daniel.

Rocking and observing him in the warm glow from the fire, she thought back over the events that had brought them here. Taken one at a time they were unlikely. Together they were unbelievable. From the initial call to help a wounded hermit to the hospital escape to the race in her truck and even the confrontation in the immense parking lot, it had been an amazing adventure.

One that actually began years ago. If she and Daniel hadn't been acquainted in the past, if she hadn't felt she owed him long-delayed thanks, she wouldn't have gone to his room to check on him and wouldn't have been there when Letty tried to trick him.

Hey, when a plan came together, it came together, she mused, smiling. A soft chuckle escaped unbidden and her patient stirred.

Kaitlin went to him and laid a hand lightly on his forehead. "How are you feeling?"

"Like I was run over by a train and didn't hear the whistles," he said. "How long was I out?"

"Seven logs and a little more kindling," she said. "It's almost time for more meds."

"Then it must be almost dawn." He started to try to sit up, reeled and fell back.

"Don't push it," Kaitlin warned. "There's no reason to hurry. While you were out I checked the storage areas and did find juice. Some bottled water, too, although it probably tastes like plastic if it's been sitting here too long, particularly during the hot summer."

"Better that than nothing."

"That's what I figured. Can I bring you a drink?"

"Sure."

Returning with one of the smaller bottles she'd bought herself, she found him once again asleep. The time on her phone indicated at least another forty-five minutes before she'd need to dose him again so she returned to the rocker to sit. And wait. And watch. And pray. Exhaustion insisted she shut her eyes. Just for a moment.

Kaitlin didn't know she'd fallen asleep until she heard Daniel shout, as if his pain had pushed him over the edge of reason and into hysteria.

Reality vanished. The cement floor beneath his body was icy cold. Gritty. Daniel was finally alone in the abandoned warehouse but had been bound, hand and foot, and gagged. His captors had taken turns beating him, then trussed him up before going to pick up others and celebrate, apparently believing he was either deceased or soon would be.

Struggling to take a deep breath, he felt sharp pains in his side. Parting kicks when he'd been down and helpless had probably broken ribs. Not that such injuries were his biggest problem. He'd heard them discussing his fate. He knew the worst.

Heart pounding, he struggled against his bonds. Couldn't move. Had they broken his leg, too? Something was causing worse agony near his left knee than anywhere else.

Blackness came and went as he fought unseen foes. Broke loose. Scrambled across the littered floor, pulled himself up and ran for his life.

Initially, Kaitlin tried to keep the blanket tucked around Daniel. She failed. Not only were his arms flailing, he was kicking with both legs despite obvious pain. She had to make him stop.

"Daniel!"

A muscular, swinging arm caught her across the shoulder and sent her to the floor. She bounced up. Tried again. "Daniel! Wake up!"

Shouts, cries, gasping. He wasn't conscious, yet his body was in full battle fury.

Kaitlin ducked twice more before she was able to get close enough to throw her arms around his neck and shout his name in his ear.

Results weren't immediate. As he continued to gasp for breath and his resistance dropped he began to weep.

Unsure of what to do, she stayed where she was, changing to murmured reassurances once he stopped trying to knock her away. "Shush. It's okay, Daniel. You're okay. I've got you."

And she did. On her knees beside him she pressed her cheek to his, absorbing some of his tears with her hair and murmuring soothing words. His shoulders shook with sobs. His arms encircled and held her as if she were his only life-line.

Kaitlin supposed his nightmare had been brought on by the fever and didn't begrudge him the comfort of her embrace. She was drawing strength from it, as well, she realized. The only thing that truly bothered her was seeing his tears. Once he became fully aware of what was going on, she was positive he'd be mortified.

The sobs waned, replaced by a gulping struggle to stop. She leaned away. His eyes were open but he looked disoriented. "It's all right," she said tenderly. "You were having a nightmare."

"No." Daniel shoved her away as if she were an aggressor and swiped at his damp cheeks. "Did I…did I hurt you?"

Without thinking she touched her arm where

his swing had connected when he was blindly striking out. "No."

He pushed himself into a sitting position, his teeth gritting until he was stable. "The truth."

"Okay, I didn't duck fast enough the first time I tried to get close to you. But it's just a little bruise, if that."

"I could have done worse." Anger joined the pain in his face, his glittering eyes.

"It was the high fever," Kaitlin explained. "You were delirious, that's all. It won't happen again."

Humility and fury melded in his expression. She'd never seen him like this. For that matter, she'd never witnessed the same mood in anyone. It brought out a desire to hug him again while also warning that she'd best keep her distance.

Finally, Daniel blinked to clear his vision and looked straight at her. "It wasn't because of any fever," he said flatly. "It's a leftover condition that got me put on extended leave from my department."

"Can it keep happening?"

"Yes."

"How did it start?"

"With the kidnapping. I told you I got grabbed. What I didn't say was that even after I escaped it left me with scars you can't see. I thought I was getting better but my chief up in St. Louis disagreed when I kept thinking I was being stalked."

"But somebody is after you. I saw that for myself."

"Oh, yeah. There's a price on my head. But my flashbacks are another story. I can never tell what will set me off and I can't be responsible for what I may do when I'm like that."

"I'm so sorry, Daniel. How can I help?"

Reaching behind him, under the loose blanket, he produced the pistol he'd taken from Grainger, dropped the clip, worked the slide to clear the chamber and handed the ammunition to her. "You can hold these. I don't want to be responsible for hurting anybody by accident."

"What good is a gun with no bullets?"

"It still has shock value," Daniel insisted. "I'd give it to you if I was sure you wouldn't try to use it."

"You could give me lessons. You said I was missing that part of my education, remember?"

"Later. After we're back in civilization and I'm on my feet again. Right now, those are the only bullets we have. We can't waste them on target practice."

"And you don't intend to show me how to re-load, right?"

"Right. You're too fearless. I knew it the minute I learned that you charged into the house to rescue me after I was shot."

"Speaking of doing what I'm trained for, I'll

bring you a pan of water and a rag so you can wash up and put on clean clothes while I use the facilities outside."

"I don't like you going out there by yourself," he said, scowling.

"Well, it's do that or stick around and maybe see more of you than I care to." Kaitlin knew she was blushing so she turned away to fetch water she'd had warming next to the hearth. "This is from one of the plastic jugs. I sampled it and it truly is terrible tasting so using it to wash isn't a waste."

She eyed his bandage. "I'll change that dressing as soon as you're ready."

"I can do it."

"So can I. If we need to arrest or shoot anybody, you can be in charge. When it comes to medical matters, I'm the boss."

"Well, when you put it that way..."

As soon as she'd brought him clean clothing she turned on her heel and made for the door. A patient on an ambulance run wouldn't embarrass her a bit. This was different. It had become personal in less than two days and she didn't know why, other than the pressure and camaraderie they'd felt while trying to stay alive. Was that enough to bring about such a profound change in her feelings? *Apparently*, she mused, using the light on her phone to help illuminate her path.

Dawn was beginning to send rays of orange

and golden light into the sky beyond the trees, creating a warm glow among the darker trunks and sparse leaves. Now that fall had come, only cedars retained their year-round, conical shape.

A forest she had assumed would be deathly quiet was, instead, filled with odd noises and tweets and rustling.

Kaitlin was almost back to the resort building when she heard a hiss. Background noises ceased. Freezing in place, she expected to see a snake. Seconds later she realize that most reptiles would be hibernating in the nippy weather.

So what had hissed? And what was now making a chirping sound that was far too loud and frightening to come from any bird, no matter how big.

Slowly, cautiously, she began to play the thin beam of her light across surrounding undergrowth. Pairs of tiny green dots appeared close to the ground. They had to be the eyes of raccoons. Kaitlin smiled. "Hello, little guys. Sorry if I scared you."

Expecting them to run from her she was surprised to see them all look up and to one side, then take off in the opposite direction, disappearing behind the main building.

Although their fear was contagious, curiosity was enough to cause her to pause and raise the light beam. It wasn't strong. It didn't travel far. But she saw enough.

Large yellow orbs looked down from the branches of a tree she'd passed directly beneath. The panting stopped. The yellow-gold eyes widened.

Kaitlin didn't know whether to run or stand very still. What she had interpreted as odd bird chirping resumed and she could tell it was coming from the open mouth of the tawny predator.

Right then, right there, she would have traded another faceoff with assassins for this one with a mountain lion.

Should she yell? Run? Stay put and wait for Daniel to miss her and come looking? Disgusted, she remembered that she had all the ammunition in her pockets. Talk about useless.

The light on her phone dimmed so she clicked it off to save battery power. Not that it mattered. If that beast charged she wasn't going to have time to call anybody.

She did, however, remember the Daniel of the Bible and his survival in the lion's den where he'd been thrown as punishment. A whisper lodged in her throat.

The big cat shifted. The branch groaned.

Kaitlin said, "Jesus, help me," just as a sharp crack echoed like a gunshot. Branch, lion and smaller twigs hit the ground in a jumble.

She didn't wait to see what was going to happen next. Screaming Daniel's name at the top of her lungs she bolted for the porch, pounding across its wobbly boards to the front door.

Her hand was out, groping for the knob when it was jerked away. Daniel stood in the gap, his rustic cane raised to defend her.

"Lion!" Kaitlin screeched, shoving him backward so she could slam the door behind her, then falling into his arms, as grateful as if he'd fought off the beast bare-handed.

Tears streaked her cheeks and she was trembling from head to toe, giving thanks that he was holding her so she wouldn't collapse in a heap.

After what seemed like hours, yet was likely only minutes, Kaitlin raised her head to look up at him. "Scary."

"I gathered. Are you sure? It's easy to imagine things in an unfamiliar place like the woods."

"I'm sure."

"Okay, how did you manage to outrun it?"

Still breathing hard and shaking so badly her teeth chattered, she said, "I think… I think…"

"What?"

"I think God knocked it out of a tree." Grasping for the right words she went on, "I saw the lion above me. A branch broke and he fell before he could pounce."

Instead of doubting her conclusion or arguing

the finer points of the frightening experience, Daniel pulled her closer and held tight. That was just fine with Kaitlin. More than fine. It was perfect.

If she never received another hug for the rest of her life she wouldn't care. She'd had the best already.

A scratching noise outside caused her to cling to him more tightly. "Do you think it's trying to get in?"

"If it was full grown and determined to have you and me for breakfast, a regular wooden door wouldn't slow it down much." Cupping her shoulders with one arm he held out the other hand. "Bullets."

"You're not going to shoot it, are you?"

"If it comes through that door or one of these boarded windows you'd better believe I'm going to do something. A loud bang should be enough to scare it away."

"And waste a bullet?"

Daniel expertly loaded the gun and chambered a live round. "This is cop stuff. That means I'm in charge."

"I'm the one who was on the menu." Leaving him she hurried to the kitchen and was back in a flash with a couple of large pots. "Hang on."

Holding each by its handle she banged them together repeatedly, then stopped to listen. "Ta-da! No more scratching."

The slow shaking of his head and a murmur of "Unbelievable" tickled her enough to bring a nervous laugh.

Cane in one hand, pistol in the other, Daniel approached. "We ought to make sure."

"You're not going to open that, are you? Stop. I want to change the rules. This incident does not fall into the category of police business."

"Well, it sure isn't medical. At least not yet." Gesturing with the pistol and keeping it pointed at the ceiling for safety, he leaned on the wall next to the door to free up one hand. "Stand clear."

Kaitlin did better than that. She armed herself with the fireplace poker and waited across the room. When she heard him begin to chuckle she lowered her weapon. "What's so funny?"

"Muddy, wet prints on the porch are from raccoons. You probably scared the life out of them."

"I saw those, too, a whole family of them. They took one look at the lion and ran. Probably came here looking for a place to hide."

"Whatever you say. You dropped your phone out there in the yard. Want me to stand guard while you go get it?"

"No, thanks. If it's still there when we leave I may pick it up. Otherwise, I'm not interested."

"You really are scared, aren't you?"

"Do EMTs use stethoscopes? Of course I'm scared. There was a real live cougar out there, just like the ones on the TV nature programs. Raccoons are little furry guys with tiny hands, pointy noses and brown-and-white rings around their tails. Lions are big and tan and make funny noises."

"What kind of noises?"

Kaitlin fisted her hands on her hips and stood firm to face him. "It wasn't a roar. I've never heard anything like it before. It sounded like this." She demonstrated by forcing air through her half-closed mouth and adding a bit of a squeaky throat sound to it.

Daniel mimicked her, only his rendition was closer to reality.

"That's it!"

"They call it a chirp."

Instead of continuing to dismiss her reported sighting he crossed the room and folded her into another embrace. She didn't need him to say a word. His actions and expression told her everything important. Not only was he saying she had been right, he was plainly grateful and astounded that she had come through the encounter unscathed.

Kaitlin didn't care whether or not the cat had simply chosen a weak limb or had been knocked down. All she knew was that she was safe again.

And that Daniel was bestowing another of the amazing hugs she was getting all too used to.

It was almost—*almost*—worth what she had just been through.

TWELVE

Daniel was loathe to delay for long after the breaking of his fever, particularly because he didn't want Kaitlin to see another example of his mental distress. Nevertheless, he came to the conclusion he wouldn't be worth a penny if he was unable to defend her, should it come to that.

One thing he didn't want to do, however, was linger at the abandoned lodge a second longer than necessary. It had provided shelter in the storm but the morning was sunny and a lot warmer. He was ready to hit the road.

Kaitlin handed him a mug with brown liquid in it, explaining when he didn't immediately drink. "That's coffee."

"Are you sure?"

"Relatively sure. I did the best I could with the water I'd been warming by the fire."

"We let the fire burn out."

"Which is why your instant coffee looks a little funny."

Amused by her efforts if not the result, he took a tentative sip. "Looks aren't everything. It tastes funny, too."

"Picky, picky, picky."

"So you've told me before." Glancing from the mug to her, he asked, "Where's yours?"

"I'm not a coffee drinker."

"Since when?"

The expression on her pretty face was telling even before she said, "Since this morning."

Taking one more sip he wrinkled his brow. "Thought so." Then he paused until she started to smile before adding, "The best part about this is the hint of plastic flavor."

"There wasn't any creamer or sugar in the kitchen to mask it." Kaitlin grinned at him. "Bon appétit."

Chuckling, he raised his mug in a mock toast. "Is that French for drink it or else?"

"Something like that."

As soon as she turned away he dashed the tepid liquid into the fireplace to finish quenching the last embers. If Kaitlin heard the splash she didn't acknowledge it. She did whirl and stare at him when he said, "Pack up. It's time to hit the road."

"No."

"What do you mean, no?"

"I mean no. No way. No how. You're not strong

enough to travel yet. There's still redness around your wound. The infection isn't gone."

"My fever broke."

"This time it did. Get too tired or stressed and you can be flat on your back again."

"I have antibiotics left. I'll keep taking them."

Fisting her hands on her hips she stood firm, chin out, eyes narrowing with determination. "You certainly will. And you will continue to rest for at least one more day. Medical decision. Mine."

"We still have to move," Daniel said, nodding assent with reservations. "I only brought us here because I knew how sick I was and the storm caught us unprepared."

"Where else can we go?"

"A campground, maybe? I don't know. We can skirt the shore of the lake till we come to one. How much cash is left?"

"Very little."

It pained him to see her discouraged. "Then a motel is out no matter how much I need a shower."

"I did rinse out a few things last night while you were sleeping. We'll make do."

"Are you for real?"

Kaitlin arched an eyebrow at him. Her smile was lopsided with muted humor. "Because?"

"Because you're so agreeable. Most women would be ranting about having to stop here at all, not to mention insisting on having all the amenities of a posh hotel and restaurant meals."

"I am *not* most women," she countered.

That made Daniel laugh and shake his head. "Lady, you can say that again."

"All right. I'm not like..."

He waved a hand to stop her and continued chuckling. "Yeah, I get it. Know what you remind me of? A pioneer. This is obviously all new to you, yet you've adjusted and coped."

She sobered. "All except about the mountain lion. I didn't do well when that happened."

"Sure you did." Although he wanted to go to her, to embrace her again at the mere remembrance of the close call, he held himself in check. "You survived."

"I wonder if my cell phone did."

"We'll soon find out. The battery may have run down, though."

"I keep a charger in the truck," Kaitlin said proudly. "Never can tell when I'll need it."

"Do you have many more surprises in store for me?" he quipped.

When Kaitlin replied, "You'd be surprised," he would have laughed again if she hadn't looked so serious.

What occurred to him next wiped away all amusement. "Uh-oh."

"What now?"

"If anybody knows you and I are together they can track us through your phone."

"They may know you have a partner but how would they know who I am?"

"The license on your truck? The contact we'd had before you rolled me out of the hospital? Any number of ways."

"That's not good."

"No, it isn't." Daniel began to gather up the supplies nearest to him, continuing to lean on the cane so he wouldn't stress his leg. "Go pack up all you can grab. We need to hit the road ASAP."

"You don't really think anybody will follow us all the way up here, do you? We heard raccoons on the porch. Surely we'd have heard a car."

"Not if they parked by the highway to wait for us."

"If you're trying to scare me, it's working," Kaitlin said.

"I'm trying to think ahead like someone determined to track me down and collect bounty money," he said gruffly. "The sooner we get out of here, the more likely I am to live long enough to get back to St. Louis and put an end to this vendetta."

"That's the first time you've used that word."

Daniel froze with the blanket over his arm and stared at her. "It's the first time I've thought of it that way. But that may be the answer I've been looking for."

"What do you mean?"

"All along it's seemed strange to me that anybody would care if I got away after taking such a bad beating. I mean, the punishment had been delivered, the message sent, yet right after that things started happening. For instance, a few weeks later, Levi was ambushed coming out of Letty's place. She's positive he was shot because he was mistaken for me, which is why she's gone over to the other side."

Kaitlin was shaking her head. "That makes no sense. If she thought the gang you infiltrated was responsible for his murder, why join forces with those same guys? It's them she should hate, not you."

"Good point. If we hadn't had to run from her and her cohorts twice I might consider that idea valid. But remember the hospital? The way she tried to lead me into a trap?"

"I'm not likely to forget. That was a close one."

"So was Springfield. I'd thought I could trust Anthony Grainger to help me until I spotted Letty and heard him call out to her. She's in this up to her neck."

"You still haven't given me a good reason why they want you dead." Kaitlin crossed her arms and shivered as she spoke.

"The raid. After I escaped and told my chief what had happened, SWAT raided the home of the gang's leader. He escaped but one of his nephews was wounded and later passed away. I hadn't made that connection before but it makes perfect sense. This is more than a hit on a cop. My subconscious solved the mystery of why when *vendetta* came to me."

"Which means they aren't likely to call off the hunt," Kaitlin concluded.

"No, they aren't." Doubling his efforts, Daniel limped over to the sofa and collected the trash they had failed to burn when they could have. "We need to pick up every sign we were ever here and wipe the place down for fingerprints, just in case the ones who follow our trail happen to be law enforcement."

"You don't trust anybody?"

"Not at the moment," Daniel told her. "Even if there are only a couple of turncoats on the force, the rest of them are looking for me, too, hoping to bring me in for protective custody. Once that happens I'll be as defenseless as I was in the hospital unless we can identify the bad cops and have them dealt with first."

"And you plan to do that how?"

Daniel didn't answer her. He had no idea how he was going to win each battle, let alone the war.

* * *

Kaitlin would have loved to check the muddy yard for the large paw prints of the cougar but decided to squelch curiosity in favor of good sense. She smiled to herself, proud of the sensible choice.

Another thing she and Daniel had discussed was the destruction of her poor, soggy phone. He had her stop the truck next to where it lay so he could remove the battery, then back up and run over it, squashing its remains into the sticky goo.

There was mud on his sandals when he pulled himself back into the passenger side and slammed the door. "Done. There's no way we can erase what they may already know but we can't be tracked any farther."

"You're only guessing they've figured out who I am. Why did we have to kill my poor phone?"

"Because I was too feverish and out of it last night to think clearly and remove the battery. I'm sorry about your phone. When all this is over I'll get you a new one."

"Pink. With a protective case and an upgrade," Kaitlin said, hoping to draw him into a less serious conversation.

"All the whistles and bells," Daniel vowed.

"Then see that you take your pills, listen to your nurse and keep your head down," she said with a smile. "I mean to collect everything you owe me, and then some."

"Like?"

To her delight he was smiling again. A short lock of hair had curled by his forehead and shadows accentuated dimples she had failed to notice before. The more handsome he appeared, the less she wanted to chance alienating him by mentioning the fondness she was recognizing, so she grabbed at the first idea that popped into her head. "I figured there must be a reward or something involved with this escapade of ours. You can tell your chief or whoever's in charge to give it to me."

He huffed. "I didn't think you were that mercenary."

"I'm not. But I'm missing work, so I won't get paid. And the longer it takes me to finish my paramedic schooling the longer my wages will stay low. Besides the out-of-pocket cash, it's cost me a lot to keep company with you."

"Ah. Okay." He feigned wiping sweat from his brow. "I was afraid for a second there that you were asking about collecting the bounty."

Kaitlin sobered. "That's not funny."

"Sorry."

He reached across to gently pat the back of her hand where it gripped the wheel and she almost swerved. Didn't he realize how sensitive she was to his touch? Was it possible he hadn't gotten the same vibes during their embraces as she had? Possibly, she reasoned. Then again, she'd been privy to his most private struggles. Surely that had bonded them beyond casual acquaintances. It had pried open her heart as if Daniel had applied a crowbar. Theirs wasn't a simple relationship. Not anymore. And as far as Kaitlin was concerned, it would never return to the way it had been when they'd met again after so long.

Because I know I owe him my life, she affirmed silently. Memories of her teenage struggles almost brought tears to her eyes. If he had failed to use discretion that night when her street friends had been arrested, she could easily have gone to jail and spent the rest of her life trying to find her way again.

"I will never, ever, betray you," she told him. "Never."

His fingers curled over hers, warm and gentle. When he said, "I know," the moisture she'd been denying blurred her vision. She blinked. A few tears spilled out and trickled down her cheeks.

He shifted, trying to move closer, and made a guttural sound as pain interfered. Instead, he released her hand and used the backs of his fingers to dry her cheeks.

The effort was so loving, so tender, it brought more weeping. She wasn't sad, she was touched so deeply, so poignantly, the tears simply came.

Apparently Daniel realized what was happening because he said, "Hey, don't cry, partner. If the new phone isn't enough, I'll buy you a pony."

That helped. Kaitlin sniffled and glanced over at him. "A what?"

"A pony. Or a puppy if you don't have room to keep a horse where you live."

"You are a crazy man, you know that?"

"And you love every nutty thing I do and say. Right?"

The reference to loving something almost caused her to blurt out too much truth. At the last second she regained control and came up with the perfect retort.

"Cashews are my favorite nut. That's what I should call you. Would you like that nickname?"

Daniel chortled and leaned back against the seat. "Not unless you want me to come up with one for you. I was thinking Bonnie to my Clyde."

"No good." Tears gone, Kaitlin was grinning. "Maid Marion to your Robin Hood?"

"No bow and arrow. And no band of merry men. Sorry."

"Well, we're not going to be Juliet and Romeo. You know how they ended up."

"Um-hum." A hint of tenderness had entered his voice.

Kaitlin blushed. "Forget I mentioned it. No nicknames."

"Oh, I don't know. If I think of the perfect one we may have to renegotiate."

"We can talk about that later," Kaitlin said. "We're coming up to the highway. Keep your eyes open for an ambush."

"Butch and Sundance," Daniel offered.

She was glad to see him leaning forward and checking the upcoming highway despite his continued teasing.

There was no visible traffic coming. And no cars or SUVs were parked along the road, waiting for them.

Kaitlin wheeled onto the pavement and accelerated, freed of worry for the present. "Whew! Lookin' good."

Lack of a reply caused her to shoot a quick look at her passenger. "What's wrong?"

"Probably nothing," Daniel said, although there was concern in his expression that she didn't understand.

"But…"

He sighed. "But when we left the dirt, I could see two fresh sets of tire tracks in the mud. They must have been made after it stopped raining."

"During the night, then."

"Yes."

Kaitlin's hands tightened on the steering wheel as her brain fought to suggest dire scenarios. She refused to listen. Anyone could have pulled off to rest or ride out the worst of the storm. The tire impressions didn't have to have been made by their enemies.

But they certainly could have been. She countered her own thought. *They certainly could have been.* But now that her cell phone was no longer sending signals, whoever might be tracking them that way would have to find another method, starting with visual contact.

Had Daniel thought of that? she wondered. It didn't really matter if he had because they couldn't go back and change anything.

Whatever was out there, whatever lay ahead, they were going to have to meet it head-on and take their chances once again.

THIRTEEN

The disadvantage of the winding, narrow road skirting the lake was the difficulty of telling whether they were being followed. The advantage was that a pursuer couldn't see far ahead, either. If they turned off quickly there was a fair chance of at least temporary respite. Did he think the tire tracks in the mud were suspicious? *Oh, yeah.*

Daniel racked his brain. He'd been up in that area before, but at that time his mind had been busy working out a different kind of survival puzzle. Pretending to be a crook to fool others wasn't the same as trying to outthink those same people. Plus, he didn't know them all by sight so a seemingly innocent civilian might turn out to be a deadly enemy.

Once he had infiltrated the criminal organization he'd realized it was far more widespread than law enforcement had first thought. Its arms extended like the many-fingered lake they were skirting, from St. Louis all the way down to

Springfield. His work and ensuing arrests had dismantled large portions of the monster but it wasn't dead yet. And as long as there was money left with which to hire mercenaries, the threat remained.

And speaking of threats… He leaned to peer into the outside mirror, waiting for the next bend in the road to show him what lay behind. Perhaps the flash of light he'd thought he noticed wasn't from the sun reflecting off another vehicle, after all. Or maybe it was. Until Kaitlin rounded another S curve he couldn't be certain either way.

All he said was, "Faster."

"Do you see something?"

"I thought I did. Can't tell now." He loosened his seat belt and lifted his sore leg with both hands so he could twist more easily to look directly at the road behind.

"What do you want me to do?" Kaitlin asked.

"Look for a side road."

"And turn? Without knowing where it goes?"

"You stuck with me the last time."

"True. But the faster I drive, the less likely I'll spot a turnoff in time."

Her constant contrariness got to him. "Deal with it," he snapped.

"All right, all right. You don't have to bite my head off."

Daniel knew he'd been too harsh. He also knew

this was not the time to lower his guard and concentrate on smoothing her ruffled feathers. Later, when they were relatively safe again, he'd consider apologizing, assuming she was still miffed.

A catch of breath grabbed him enough that he made a sound audible over the roar of the engine.

Kaitlin reacted immediately. "You saw something."

"Yes. I was looking for a black SUV. The vehicle gaining on us is a lighter color, maybe tan or white."

"Then how do you know it's after us?"

"The speed, for one thing. Nobody but a hit man or teenage boy drives like that up here."

"Hah! You have *me* driving like that."

"You're different."

"You can say that again." Kaitlin braked suddenly. Daniel would have slid off the seat if he hadn't kept the seat belt on.

Momentum pinned him to the truck door. He grabbed for the dash to brace himself and looked ahead. She'd spotted a turnoff. "Next time warn me."

"Next time, pay attention," she shot back.

He had to admit that her skills behind the wheel were superb. Police officers took classes in defensive driving. Kaitlin seemed to have developed the ability naturally.

Another bump and jolt. "Ouch."

"I'll slow down in a second," she promised. "I didn't know this would be so rough."

"And muddy. If they spot our tracks and follow, we'll need an escape plan."

"One catastrophe at a time is my limit."

Before Daniel had a chance to point out a side shoot from the narrow track, she'd seen it and was turning again. "Good."

"Glad you approve." The firm tone was evidence she was still upset with him.

"Look, I'm sorry I snapped at you, okay?"

"We're both wound tighter than a tourniquet so you're forgiven. How's the leg?"

"I—I'd forgotten all about it." Daniel knew his shortness of breath and slightly halting speech contradicted that statement, but he figured Kaitlin wouldn't argue when she was preoccupied with her driving. Wherever she was taking them, it had to be better than staying on the main highway. At least he hoped so, because at this point they were committed.

"I'm going to keep going until I run out of road or find a place to turn around," she said. "That okay with you?"

"You're the boss."

To his astonishment she started to smile. "I was wondering. This isn't medical or police work but it's kind of closer to what you do."

"Being in control is a big deal to you, isn't it?"

Kaitlin nodded as she slowed their pace and maneuvered between rows of saplings crowding the sides of the muddy trail. "Yes, it is. I'd be an unhappy doctor instead of a satisfied EMT if I hadn't learned to take charge of my life."

"That's not a bad thing as long as you don't take it to extremes." Speaking before realizing that she would certainly consider his opinion criticism, Daniel waited for backlash. Instead, he got agreement—of sorts.

"I've been trying to teach myself that everybody isn't out to run my life," Kaitlin said, pausing to ease into a tight turn, then continuing. "It's a hard habit to break. I have to find ways to stand up for what I believe, what I want, without alienating everyone who cares about me."

His initial reaction was to picture himself as the subject of her observation. That notion was dashed when she said, "Take my paramedic friend, Vince Babcock. He's the one who told me to wait instead of busting into your house to stop your bleeding. I know I drive him crazy most of the time. I'm just hoping he starts to see value in my instincts soon."

"Vince?"

"Older guy. Dark hair. Always grumpy. You met him when you called our ambulance."

"Can't say I remember. I was pretty out of it then." Thankful that Kaitlin's description of the paramedic didn't sound complimentary, Daniel started to view himself as a person who was willing to let her be herself.

"I may be a tad impetuous at times, but you have to admit it's been beneficial. Can you imagine a woman like Letty pushing you out of the hospital in a wheelchair as if the place was on fire?" She chuckled. "I wish I could have stood back and watched us. I'm sure we were pretty awesome."

"You were," Daniel told her. "I have to admit you're unique."

"That's good, right?"

"Oh, yeah." He had to grin despite their awkward situation. "You are definitely one of a kind." More softly he added, "And I'm thankful."

Mirroring his smile she brought the truck to a stop so she could look directly at him. "Me, too. I've never had this much fun before, not counting being scared out of my wits half the time. I'll be relieved when I get you back to St. Louis, but I am going to miss our adventures."

Partly amused, Daniel was nonetheless deeply concerned. "Don't lose sight of the seriousness of all this," he warned, taking her hand. Her slim fingers were cold compared to his so he instinctively began to caress them. "We've been only a few steps ahead of the evil that's trailing us. One error, one little mistake, and we can lose this battle. Never forget that. Not for a second."

Although Kaitlin nodded, she seemed mostly focused on their joined hands. Did she truly comprehend what they were up against? He doubted it. Yes, she was courageous. And resilient. But she was also untrained in hand-to-hand self-defense and gun handling. If anything happened to incapacitate him, she'd be as vulnerable as a whitetail deer standing in the middle of a busy highway and too stunned to jump out of the way of speeding cars.

Resolve filled him. It was too late to exclude her from his troubles, not that she'd back off even if he begged. But it wasn't too late to teach her a few basic things before they returned to the highway.

"Find a clearing near here, if you can," Daniel said. "We're making temporary camp."

"We're what?"

"You heard me. One more night isn't going to matter in the long run, and staying hidden will throw off whoever has been tracking us. We can make them think we're way ahead or maybe crossed to the opposite side of the lake."

"Because nobody will believe a smart cop like you would park himself in the middle of nowhere, wounded and vulnerable, when he could be making tracks for safety?"

"Yeah. Something like that." He quirked a smile. "Are you with me?"

Kaitlin rolled her eyes. "Where else would I be?"

His initial urge was to praise her with a comment he'd had to school himself to quit using, given most modern women's prejudices, but he dearly wanted to pat her hand and say, "Good girl."

Kaitlin wasn't about to show Daniel how happy she was to have the opportunity to spend more time with him, so she carefully schooled her features, especially any time he was looking her direction.

The spot they finally chose was more of a clearing than an actual camping area. "I wish you'd put a tent on the shopping list," Kaitlin remarked.

"If I had you'd have run out of cash before you bought anything else."

"There is that. Remind me, next time I go on the lam, to plan ahead and save up more getaway money."

"Same could be said for me."

She hadn't meant to depress him, not for a second, so she kept talking. "This is kind of like those survival shows on TV. We get dumped in the mountains and have to fend for ourselves." Purposely smiling at him she said, "If you try to make me eat grubs or insects we are through, you hear me?"

"Insects can't be worse than those glued-together nuts and berries you bought."

"Talk about being picky."

"Don't knock it if you haven't tried it. When I find a nice, tasty grub I may even share."

Kaitlin chuckled. "If you find a nice tasty grub I'll want to watch you swallow it." Pretending a shiver of distaste, she made a face at him. "Ugh."

He had joined her at the rear of the truck and was leaning on the cane, averting his face whenever he shifted position. She was sure he was grimacing in pain, even though he was doing his best to hide it.

"Before we make camp I want to check your leg and change the bandage. We had a wild ride," Kaitlin said.

"The leg is fine."

"Calling medical control on this one," she said firmly as she let down the tailgate and pointed. "Sit."

"Metal's cold."

"You should try being stuck in a sleeveless top. I don't dare wear my uniform shirt because it has my name on it."

Kaitlin hadn't meant to complain but Daniel heard it that way. "I'm sorry. I wish I had something of value to sell so I could take better care of you."

For a split second she took offense. That was enough to make her rip loose the last piece of tape.

"Ow." He was rubbing his leg. "You did that on purpose."

"It slipped."

"No, you slipped," he countered, almost smiling enough that she could feel relieved. "You had a gut-level reaction to what I said and didn't stop yourself in time."

Shaking her head she tried to mask a smile. "The more time I spend with you, the smarter you get. I must be a good influence."

"You are amazing," he said with a tenderness she didn't expect to hear right then.

Instead of throwing her arms around him and delivering a similar compliment, she chose to rely on her wit. "And don't you forget it."

Gentle fingers checked his wound, then bandaged it again. "Keep taking your pills for a couple more days, at least. By then we should be back in civilization where you can get proper medical care."

"You're doing fine."

"Humph. I'm doing first aid, not the job a paramedic could do."

"You'll be one soon, right?"

She concentrated on the bandaging rather than meeting his questioning gaze. "Right. All I have to do is pass an impossibly hard written test and the practical exam in the field. Piece of cake."

"Speaking of food, aren't you hungry?"

"Why? Did you spot a creepy-crawly?"

"Not yet. I figured to nibble on nuts and berries until I do." He gingerly slid off the tailgate and stood. "The leg really does feel better. Honest."

"It looks better, too." She was scanning the clearing. "How in the world are we going to make ourselves comfortable here? It looks like the edge of a swamp."

"If the sun doesn't dry the ground enough, I can bunk in the truck bed while you sleep in the cab."

"Medical control again. You belong inside. I'll be fine out here."

"I'm too tall to stretch out in the truck," Daniel countered. "Besides, there's only one blanket."

"And a couple of smaller reflective covers." Kaitlin couldn't help blushing. "I never dreamed we'd be stuck in the woods this long or I'd have bought two full-size blankets."

"We need a knife," he said.

"Mags gave me bandage scissors. Why?"

"To split the blanket."

Kaitlin didn't appreciate his satisfied grin but she was on board with sharing the only warmth in an acceptable way. "Thanks for not assuming I'd be willing to sleep with you."

"Who says I'm doing this for you?" The grin widened.

"I just figured you understood I wasn't that kind of person. I mean, I have mentioned God more than once."

"Hey. We're on the same team," Daniel said. "You should have figured *that* out by now."

"It's not only because of my Christian faith," she said flatly. "I don't do things like that. Not since…"

"I know. I remember that confused teenage girl you used to be. It's okay. We all get lost from time to time. That doesn't mean we can't start over."

"I have, you know."

She was relieved to see total acceptance in his expression. When he said, "I know," with such conviction and tenderness, it was almost enough to make her weep. She bit back tears and purposely switched her focus.

"Okay. Since I know nothing about camping other than roasting marshmallows on a stick, and we currently have no marshmallows, you're in charge of whatever we need to do next. Anything that involves walking I can do for you."

"Are you up to gathering firewood? We'll need to spread it out in a patch of sun and let it dry all day if we hope to have a warming fire tonight."

She was eyeing the woods. "Um, sure."

"Mountain lions and raccoons are nocturnal," he teased.

"Says you. I wish I knew how to shoot."

"Because you forgot to bring those loud cooking pots to bang together?"

"Yes."

"Don't worry. The wildlife is more scared of you than you are of them." He hobbled over to the edge of the clearing and picked up a chunk of dead wood. "I don't think you'll have to go far to find all we need. There's plenty like this close by."

"Right. And I did volunteer." She made a silly face to bolster her own courage and amuse him. "That'll teach me to keep my mouth shut."

Daniel began to laugh. Kaitlin faced him, hands on her hips. "What's so funny?"

When he finally regained enough control to speak he said, "The idea that anything will teach you to keep quiet."

"Ha-ha." Her raised hand halted his laughing. "With all the noise you're making, mister, let's hope nobody else turned off the highway. We'll be easy to find if they did. All they'll have to do is follow the sound."

All she'd wanted was to squelch the personal joke, but then she realized there was far more truth to her warning than was comfortable. Sight wasn't their only problem. Sound was, too. And it echoed for long distances.

Animals might be frightened.

Deer hunters might be upset.

Hunters of men would be delighted.

FOURTEEN

If Daniel had thought he could get away with fooling Kaitlin he wouldn't have divided the blanket evenly. Giving her the larger piece would have been a magnanimous gesture but getting that difference past her keen eyes and controlling nature would be next to impossible, so he made the split equal and added one of the reflective covers to hold in the heat.

Despite his plans to the contrary, he'd fallen asleep repeatedly during the day, thankful for the sunshine, the clearing hidden amid a thick stand of hickory and cedars, and the chance to rest and regain strength. Knowing Kaitlin would stay close to her truck to keep an eye on him gave him peace, too. She might be stubborn and opinionated but she was also smart and cautious. She wouldn't wander away, even in the daytime.

Awaking from a deep sleep, he yawned and stretched. He'd rolled all the way onto his back before he realized there was far less pain in his leg. Either it was numb because of his sleeping position or it was actually getting better.

Her face peeked over the side of the truck bed. "Good morning."

Daniel shaded his eyes to judge the position of the sun. "It looks more like late afternoon."

"It is. How was your mattress?"

"Kind of itchy but a lot better than lying on cold metal," he said, pretending to punch the cedar boughs she'd gathered to pad his makeshift pallet.

"If we'd brought a hatchet I could have cut better ones."

"Hey, I was a sick man when I made that list. You can't expect me to have thought of everything." He flashed a wry smile so she wouldn't make the mistake of taking him too seriously.

"You are looking better," Kaitlin said. "How do you feel?"

"Hungry, for a change."

One of her eyebrows lifted and she smiled. "Didn't you find the insects hiding in your bed and snack on those? I was sure you would."

"Thankfully, no." Daniel pushed himself into a sitting position and stretched, arms overhead. "Umm. That sun feels good. Maybe we should skip sleeping tonight when it's cooler and hit the road."

"Only if you intend to drive," Kaitlin replied,

yawning. "I stood guard while you slept. I'd probably doze off at the wheel."

"Fair enough. Want me to get up so you can lie here?"

"No, thanks. I prefer something a little less rustic."

"It was good enough for me," he teased.

"And I am delighted." Another yawn. "Now that I know you're better I think I'll crawl into the front and take a little nap."

"Okay by me. I'm actually feeling halfway human."

"Keep taking your antibiotic, anyway," Kaitlin said, "or the infection may flare up again."

"Right." He had begun sorting through her collection of freeze-dried meals. "Yum. What'll it be? Macaroni and cheese or desiccated pot roast with gravy?"

"You're going to heat water? Okay. I'll help you build the fire so it doesn't give off too much smoke."

"Nope. Not this time. You got everything ready and I need to move around so my muscles don't stiffen up." Sliding off the tailgate he paused to check his balance. Yes, his leg hurt plenty. No, he was not going to admit it.

She'd paused by the open door to the truck cab. "Are you sure?"

"Positive." Daniel made a silly face to reassure

her and pointed. "Go. Sleep. I'll wake you when it's time to eat."

A weary nod was the only answer he got. Watching her climb in and lie down he flipped her half of the blanket over his arm and hobbled around to hand it to her. "Here. Cover up with this, too."

"Not cold," Kaitlin murmured. Nevertheless, she took hold of one edge of the gray wool blanket and pulled it up over her shoulders.

Mission accomplished. Now he could take all the time he needed to gather up the dried wood and assemble the campfire. If Kaitlin had been watching he'd have felt he had to hurry to keep her from worrying. Since she wasn't, he could do it in spurts, resting when necessary to prevent overdoing it.

Daniel silently laughed at himself. There he was, about as useless as the unloaded gun, worrying about keeping up appearances for her sake. She wasn't going to think less of him if he showed temporary weakness, was she? Of course not. She'd already proved that when he'd had that vivid nightmare and awakened shouting.

"I'd better not forget that, either," he cautioned himself. He was not only a cop, which posed enough problems, he was also damaged goods. The desire to defeat criminals had led to a mental breakdown that he might someday recover from.

Or not. Either way, he'd still have the mind-set of a police officer, a man dedicated to righting wrongs no matter the cost.

The cost to myself, he added, ruing Kaitlin's involvement in what should have been borne on his shoulders and his alone. It was the instinct to survive that had forced him to make tough choices, he reasoned. Looking back on everything that had brought him to this point, to this place with her, he didn't see any alternatives that would not have led to his murder. It was as simple as that. And as complicated. She had been there at just the right time and he had grasped at the chance for survival.

Knowing her from their past encounter had helped, too, of course. As she'd said, she felt she owed him. That wasn't how he saw their tenuous relationship, at least, not at this point.

So, Daniel asked himself, *how do you feel about her?*

He grimaced. Bent to add to the pile of firewood he was assembling. Explored his true feelings and was astounded. His jaw dropped. His head swiveled.

All he could do was stare at the truck where Kaitlin napped. That young woman already meant more to him than anyone he'd ever dated. Ever. How could that have happened? He and Kaitlin had only been together for a few days.

Daniel paused and sighed, then reached for another piece of dead wood. "It'll be okay."

The sound of his softly spoken words made no echo, yet they returned to him for repetition, to help him convince himself.

"It will be. It'll be fine. This is almost over. Once she drives me the rest of the way, she'll be done. We won't ever have to see each other again."

Truth rolled over his spirit like the fog of a dewy morning and penetrated to the bone.

"I'm right. I know I am. It will be for the best," he insisted to himself, as if saying so would make it real enough to accept.

For once, he had to admit he didn't want to be right. As impossible as it seemed, he wanted his future to include Kaitlin North. Somehow. Sometime.

A dry branch cracked in the distance. Daniel was startled from his doldrums to focus on the here and now.

That was what he must do, he concluded logically. No happy dreams mattered if the people involved weren't alive to see them come to fruition.

Moving as fast as possible, he threw aside the wood and went to the truck, placing himself between the woods and the sleeping woman. Bare hands were no match for a rifle, but if it came to a confrontation he wasn't going down without a fight.

Standing braced, the cane held high, he waited for the sound, any sound, to tell him whether his enemies had found them and were closing in. Except for birds and the occasional squirrel, the woods were silent.

It wasn't the sun that woke Kaitlin, it was the smell of food. Because she'd hardly stirred once she'd fallen asleep, one arm had gone numb, not to mention a bothersome crick in her neck.

She pulled herself up by the steering wheel and scooted to the open door. "Um, is it dinnertime?"

"Almost."

His smile warmed her to the core and set her heart racing. *So what else is new?*

Making a face and sliding all the way out, she paused to smooth her wrinkled blue uniform pants. "I will sure be glad to get clean clothes."

"Wear one of the new shirts you bought."

"One is still damp from washing and you're wearing the second, remember?"

"Vaguely. I'm not looking forward to all your stories of what I did while I was running that high fever."

An idea made her chuckle.

"What's so funny about a fever?"

"Nothing. I wasn't laughing at that. It just occurred to me that I could tell you almost any wild story and make you believe you were out of your head and actually did it."

"You won't have to make anything up," he countered. "The real thing is bad enough."

"You're still talking about your nightmare, aren't you?" There was no doubt in her mind that that was exactly what was bothering him. Little wonder. He'd not only sounded frantic, he'd shown true fear, something a macho man like him would consider a major fault.

"Forget it. Come on over here and grab a fork. I can't believe you thought to add this cooking set."

"I was buying meals at the time. It made sense."

"That doesn't mean the average person, particularly one who had never camped, would have thought of it."

"Or made the decision to amend your list," she added with a grin. "See? There are advantages to my being such an independent woman."

It pleased her to see him stifle a laugh. "Right, providing I can overlook the times you get yourself in serious trouble by thinking too much."

"I don't think too much," Kaitlin said, reaching for the plate he was handing her. "I act too much. If all I did was come up with a wild idea and keep it to myself, you won't have a clue how helpful I can be."

"Well, start being helpful by eating that before the odor of cooking draws bears."

"I thought they were afraid of fire."

"Up to a point. They also love to raid camps and steal food that smells good to them."

"Then we should be eating granola bars," she quipped.

"Oh, they'd probably like those, too. They just wouldn't discover them inside a tight wrapper." He gestured. "I'm serious. Eat."

Kaitlin almost saluted with her fork and got gravy in her hair. She giggled and took a bite. "This tastes better than it looks. Pot roast?"

"That's what the label said. I wasn't sure when I first opened the package but the hot water helped a lot."

"I think I like it."

"Yeah, me, too." Daniel was stirring his meal with a small fork and inspecting it closely. "Although I suspect it's more pot than roast."

That brought a mutual laugh that lifted Kaitlin's spirits. A nap had been beneficial, too. "Well, whatever it is, it hits the spot. I didn't know how hungry I was until I woke up and smelled it."

"Maybe you're part bear."

"More likely I've been eating too many nuts and berries and, as you said, need real food."

"I wasn't putting down your choices," he said.

"I know. You were just wondering if you were going to starve before we got all the way to St. Louis."

"Something like that."

Good humor waning, Daniel had turned his full attention to poking at his gravy-covered meal. Clearly, he'd been happier not thinking about what might lay ahead. But somebody had to. There was going to be more to their arrival in the city than he'd revealed so far and Kaitlin wanted to know everything. Logically, if he truly did admire her intelligence he wouldn't keep her in the dark. On the other hand, if he continued to refuse to give a full explanation she'd have to assume his praise was false.

Watching him finish eating, wipe the fork clean and toss the cardboard container into the fire, Kaitlin did the same. "Sorry about forgetting marshmallows."

Daniel huffed. "No problem."

"I have a different problem," she began, hoping he'd encourage her to share her thoughts.

"Oh?"

She was nodding. "Yes. I want to know more about what you expect when we get to your chief. We need to plan."

"Can't," Daniel said gruffly as he poked the fire embers with a short piece of broken tree limb.

"Why not?" Ready to let her temper show if that was what it took, she sat back on her haunches and glowered at him.

"Because I don't have a clue what we'll find

once we get there. The hardest part will be figuring out who to trust. Ideally, I need to get past everybody at headquarters, if possible, and reach Chief Broderhaven without alerting the whole station to my presence."

"Sounds impossible. They all know you, don't they?"

"It may be worse than that," he said. "When we first figured out why Levi was killed, the chief decided to announce that I was a person of interest in that shooting. The idea was to confuse my gang connection in the hope they'd back off."

"And they didn't."

"I have no way of knowing. The price on my head is plenty of incentive to keep a lot of them searching."

"What are you worth, anyway?" As soon as he named a sum she reacted exactly as she'd planned no matter what he said. "Way too low. I'm sure you're worth at least three times that."

Daniel huffed. "Nice to know somebody appreciates me."

"Always have, always will," Kaitlin told him. "Okay, I believe you about St. Louis. We'll play it by ear."

"No, I will. Cop stuff, remember? I'm the boss."

A sidelong glance told her how serious he was about going in by himself. She wasn't going to waste breath arguing. Not yet. When the time came, however, she intended to have some kind of alternate plan ready, even if it wasn't fleshed out. After all they had been through together so far, there was no way she was going to drop him off at his headquarters and drive away.

In the meantime, they'd need to pass the time without touching on subjects that might cause dissention. That wasn't going to be easy when she knew so little about his private life. One question that had been nagging her was his personal attachments—or the lack thereof. Asking might be awkward. Not asking set her up for the ultimate in awkwardness. The more she pondered her most secret thoughts regarding this enigmatic man, the closer she came to letting herself dream.

In a way, Kaitlin almost hoped he'd dash those hopes with his answer to, "So, tell me more about yourself. I know Letty disappointed you terribly. Have you replaced her yet?"

A slight shift of his shoulders and a telling gaze proved that she'd erred. Since it was already too late to withdraw her query she decided to pursue it. "Are you seeing someone else?"

Daniel's jaw tightened, the clenching of the muscles unmistakable by firelight. "No. Are you?"

There was no verbal reply that wasn't mortifying so Kaitlin merely shook her head. If she'd said she was, he'd likely have asked for a man's name and the only one she could give, the only one that mattered even a smidgen, was Daniel Ryan.

Standing, she dusted off her clothing and did her best to look presentable before turning on her heel and heading for the truck. She had a hair-brush in her purse. And lipstick, although this cooler weather probably called for lip balm, instead.

Her idea of a perfect evening was one spent curled up in a comfy chair with a good book or maybe watching a little TV. Mysteries were her favorites. Facing those kinds of dangers in real life, however, was not the same. Not even close.

There had been instances when reading a book gave her mild jitters or a movie scene startled her enough to make her jump, but that was totally different from her life since meeting Daniel again.

This time the blood was real. The hit men were real. The guns held real bullets and the sound of a close shot was enough to make her ears hurt.

That wasn't all that hurt, either, she admitted as she climbed back into the cab of the truck and gathered her piece of blanket close for its emotional comfort as well as warmth. Her heart was breaking for him.

Kaitlin wrapped the blanket tighter, pulling her thoughts in with it. Daniel was in trouble so she'd continue to help him. Once the threats had been neutralized and he no longer needed her, she'd head for home without a backward glance and he probably wouldn't miss her.

A solitary tear slid down her cheek. She swiped it away. Her eyes might not look back when she left him in St. Louis but her heart was going to keep seeing his image as long as she lived. That wasn't a vow. It was reality.

Kaitlin didn't intend to brood if she could help it but she knew herself, inside and out. Somehow, she was going to have to find a way to keep track of him, to be certain he was alive and well whether he ever found out or not.

She shivered and gazed over at him, still hunching over the dying fire with his back to her. He had to make it through this. He had to. If anything bad happened to him she was certain she would be ready to curl up and die, too.

That conclusion made her angry, mostly at herself. Where was the strong woman who answered emergency calls and did all she could to *save* lives? Huh? What had happened to the Kaitlin North who prided herself on her hard-won independence?

What she wanted to do at that moment was vent with a wordless shout that rattled the truck windows. Instead, she sighed and shook her head. That Kaitlin, that courageous, self-confident EMT, soon to become a paramedic, had made one little mistake that had ruined everything.

How? The answer was easy. "By falling in love."

FIFTEEN

Rather than waste precious water by dousing the fire, Daniel had sat by it until the last embers died, then stirred them to make sure they wouldn't rekindle.

Under almost any other circumstances he'd be sitting there with his arm around Kaitlin's shoulders, telling her what a wonderful companion she was and suggesting they get together when all this was over, notwithstanding the fact that they lived and worked on opposite sides of the state.

No, he decided as he pushed himself to his feet; that was not going to happen. Even if he got out of this mess alive, which was plan A, there was no way he'd ask her to uproot and follow him all the way to St. Louis. She'd found her niche in a small town. Paradise was her home now.

And his goals? There was a time when he'd been certain he was on the right path, in the right job. Now? Not so much. Admitting that, however, did not mean he should abandon his own career to pursue a self-confident woman who might never decide to settle down the way he'd envisioned. Kaitlin had come from a dysfunctional family so she had no model of how a man and wife could raise happy children as well as be personally content. Her parents had fought all the time, with her trapped in the middle. No wonder she'd felt like a hapless tennis ball being batted back and forth in a game that no one ever won.

The closest Kaitlin had come to victory as a teen was her runaway life on the streets. That was another reason she'd never want to return to St. Louis. It not only held her controlling, warring parents, it was the place where she'd made her worst mistakes. At least, as far as he knew.

"I should have asked her more about her past," he muttered, starting for his makeshift bed in the back of the truck. "I should have made a stupid joke and pretended I was dating somebody who would be impossible, like a supermodel or movie star. In Hollywood maybe," he told himself. "In Missouri? I don't think so."

Besides, he reasoned, Kaitlin might half believe his wild tales and then where would he be?

"Right where I am now," he whispered.

Night birds had been singing, calling to each other from a distance. The moon gave off enough light to tell where everything was in the camp, which was advantageous since they had no other source of illumination.

Daniel started to work himself onto the bed, careful to safeguard his sore leg, then he remembered he hadn't taken his bedtime pill. Rummaging in their supplies and coming up empty he realized his meds had to be up in the cab. With Kaitlin. Who was probably sound asleep by now.

Although he did consider skipping that dose, he knew doing so was foolish. He needed to be as well and as able as possible by the time they reached their destination. No way was he messing with a schedule that was clearly working.

Abandoning the cane because he had the side of the truck to lean on, Daniel worked his way from the rear to the driver's-side door, hoping he could reach what he needed without waking his companion.

The minute the door latch snicked Kaitlin bolted upright. "What's wrong?"

"Forgot my pill. Sorry to wake you."

"I wasn't sleeping."

A sniffle caught his attention. "You catching a cold?"

"I hope not." She reached into a sack on the floor and produced the medication he needed. "Put a couple of extra in your pocket so you can take one in the middle of the night if you happen to wake up. Just be sure you drink plenty of water with it. Eat a bite, too, if you can manage to choke down part of an energy bar."

"They're not so bad." Business concluded, he knew he should slam the door and back away, but something held him there.

What should he say to her? How could he apologize for hurting her feelings without doing more damage? Deciding the situation was best left alone, he took a step back. "Well, good night again."

"Good night, Daniel."

There was so much despair in her tone his gut wrenched. Would one simple hug hurt? Oh, yeah. If he embraced Kaitlin again, feeling the way he currently did, there was no telling what might happen. He cared for her. A lot. Too much to make a misstep and ruin any chances they might have to get to know each other better in the future.

You're back on that derailed train again, are you? his brain asked. *What good is it going to do to stoke the boiler when the wheels are off the tracks?*

Disgusted with his analogy he slammed the door and was starting to turn away when he heard it. A motor. Car? Truck? A hunter on a personal transport vehicle, maybe?

He froze, straining to hear, to make up his mind where the noise originated and what it might be. It didn't occur to him that Kaitlin might be watching him until she rolled down the window and asked, "What's wrong?"

"Listen." Hand up, he gestured for her to stop and hoped she'd tell him he was imagining things.

"I do hear something. Where's it coming from?"

"Can't tell. But this white truck stands out in the moonlight like a beacon. We have to camouflage it."

"With what?"

The bed in the back caught his eye. "The branches you gathered. Help me lay them over the reflective surfaces. We can use the blankets to drape the sides if we have to."

Kaitlin not only gave him no argument, she jumped out barefoot to help. He didn't have to tell her the sound was getting louder, he could tell by her frantic movements that she knew.

When they had done the best they could, he held out his hand. "Tape. Unless you have a screwdriver."

"Not with me," she said breathlessly. "Do you need the tape for your bandage?"

"No. To cover the door switches. If we can't get the bulb out of the interior light we need to keep it from coming on when we open the doors."

"And showing whoever is out there where we are. Brilliant!" Her enthusiasm was oddly uplifting. She might be upset with him about his reluctance to share private information but she clearly admired his ingenuity.

He taped one side, then passed the roll to her and she did the other. "So far so good," Kaitlin whispered. "Now what?"

"Keys in the ignition?"

"Yes. Shall I pull them?"

"No. If we have to make a quick getaway it'll be better to have them in place."

"Shall I get back in?"

"No. Put your shoes on and grab the half blanket we didn't use for camouflage. We're going to hide in the woods."

"Oh, no."

"Oh, yes, Kaitlin. Ease your door closed. We'll watch from a hiding place. If it looks like they're getting too close, we'll decide whether to stay where we are or hop in and drive off."

"Sounds better than standing around in the dark in that creepy forest," she countered, tying her shoes.

Daniel made a command decision, one he prayed was for the best. "Give me the clip and that extra bullet for the chamber," he said, a hand held out. "I'm going to load before we leave the truck."

"Now you're making sense."

"I sure hope so," he said quietly. "I sure hope so."

* * *

Sound bounced off the irregular terrain and trees as if the vehicle they were listening for was in three or four places at once. Knowing it was an echo and accepting the presence of only one car or truck didn't help Kaitlin's nerves. She wished the section of gray blanket was a sleeping bag, with tight seams to keep out the creeping, crawling denizens of the forest. Not to mention bigger threats. Like mountain lions, for instance.

Tension pushed her closer to Daniel until he put both the blanket and an arm around her shoulders. She would gladly have complained if she hadn't been silently wishing for exactly that to happen.

"Where do you think they are now?" she whispered.

It wasn't necessary for him to lean closer to hear her, yet he did, anyway. "Sounds farther away."

"I thought so, too." That was the plain truth. It was also not nearly enough to make her duck out from under his arm. Even when she didn't feel totally safe and sure of herself she intended to act the part—except in special circumstances like this one.

Keeping up a pretense of unshakable courage wasn't only for Daniel's benefit. She needed to make herself believe they were out of immediate danger in order to function well if the need arose.

"You're shivering." His hold tightened. He pulled her closer.

"So are you." Kaitlin drew a corner of the blanket across, enfolding them both and trying to share the warmth.

"We need to get you back in the truck. You're freezing."

"You, too."

"I'll be okay standing guard."

"You are not okay *standing* anything," she argued.

"So I'll sit."

Where fear and the comfort of his closeness had not been enough to convince her to pull away, anger succeeded. "Yes, you will. Inside the cab with me. That's the only way this will work and keep both of us from getting sick."

She could see enough of his face by moonlight to tell that he was not pleased. *Well, tough.*

"The other thing we could do is hit the road," Daniel said. "Our supplies are already on board."

"How do you know killers aren't parked out there somewhere, waiting for us to show ourselves?"

"How do *you* know they won't wait all night, anyway?" Daniel asked.

"Because we were watching my truck and they never got close enough to spot it yet."

"You know this because?"

"Because they didn't stop and check out the camp. Our camouflage job worked."

Kaitlin heard him make a guttural noise that was not a distinguishable word. Nevertheless, she knew exactly what message it conveyed. Their conflict had become a battle of wills rather than being defined by cause. Common sense, which she felt was always on her side, and the practice of medicine dictated rest and caution, while police instinct was currently against staying put.

That was understandable. Daniel was a man of action. He didn't want to just sit there and wait to be discovered by the next person who might be on his trail. As far as she could discern, he was thinking like a hunter, not like prey.

"Listen, even little rabbits know enough to freeze when they're being stalked," Kaitlin said.

"And they get eaten."

"Not the ones who don't panic and bolt before the predator gives up and goes away."

"I'm not a rabbit."

"No," she said, making special effort to keep her voice calm and even-toned, "you're not. But you are who every crook in the state seems to be hunting."

"We can be spotted more easily in daylight."

"We can also see who or what is after us and escape better," Kaitlin countered. "You can't have it both ways and your leg is far from healed."

"That will take weeks and you know it."

"Make it months if you don't want to limp the rest of your life."

He snorted derisively. "Depends on how long that is."

"Which brings me back to our original problem. You'll have the best chance—we both will—of making it to your chief in one piece if you're alert and rested."

Instead of answering, he grabbed her hand and pulled her back toward the clearing. Reaching the truck, he jerked open the door, tossed the blanket in first, then literally lifted her to the edge of the seat and dropped her there.

Kaitlin put up with the macho act that far. When he took a step back and tried to close the door she balked. "No. No way. You get in here and keep warm or I'll be out the other door faster than you can get around to stop me."

"Don't be ridiculous."

"You're the ridiculous one." Her lips pressed into a thin line and she pointed at him. "Look at yourself and use a little common sense. You're hurt. You've had a fever that has only recently broken. Everything you do that uses your sore leg not only taxes your stamina, it sets you up to reopen the wound. Then you'll be ripe for another, worse infection on top of the initial one." She scooted away from the door to make room. "So, what'll it be? My way or the wrong way?"

As she observed him and judged what kinds of ideas might be spinning through his brain, she sensed a partial change. Perhaps a softening. At least she hoped so.

"All right," Daniel began, "this is how it will go."

Kaitlin almost stopped him right there. Discretion slowed her negative response enough for him to finish expressing his thoughts.

"We'll wait until just before dawn and try to get some rest in the meantime, even if we can't sleep sitting up. As soon as the sky starts to lighten we'll be on our way whether we feel ready or not. Clear?"

"As a bell," Kaitlin said, holding back her reservations. She wasn't afraid of sharing the cab of the truck with him. After all, they'd been in those same circumstances ever since leaving the hospital and he'd been a perfect gentleman. Any plan that resulted in his sleeping, even fitfully, was okay with her. It wasn't as if they were romantically involved.

She shoved aside the small cooler and scooted over farther to give him as much foot room as possible. Elevation would be best, of course, but that wasn't possible. Or was it?

The moment she reached past the cooler for the door handle he grasped and held her other wrist.

"I'm not running off. I promise. I just want to move the cooler into the back to give us more room."

"Okay. Sorry. I thought…"

"I know. You're all keyed up and ready to suspect betrayal from all sides." Sighing, she touched his forearm before opening the driver's door. "I will never turn against you, Daniel. You have my word."

Tension visibly left him. He nodded and leaned his head to the side, resting it and his shoulder against the closed passenger door.

As soon as Kaitlin returned she shoved a small bag of clothing at him. "Put this behind you as a pillow and turn to face me."

"Why?"

"Because you're going to put your foot in my lap. We need to get that leg up or it'll swell more than before."

"I should argue with you," he said, "but I'm too tired."

Grimacing and biting back groans, he did as she'd instructed. Kaitlin quickly discovered that wasn't the most comfortable position for her, yet made up her mind to tolerate it for as long as possible. She removed his sandal and dropped it on the floor, then turned the blanket segment sideways and spread it out to cover them both.

Daniel gathered his portion close and closed his eyes.

Kaitlin was still awake when his breathing slowed and deepened. Listening to that steady rhythm lulled her and finally brought much needed sleep to her, too.

SIXTEEN

Sunshine warming his face through the windows woke Daniel. Ready to snap at Kaitlin for letting him oversleep he saw that she was asleep, too. As soon as he tried to lift his leg she stirred.

"Sorry. I didn't mean to disturb you."

"Did so. You wanted to be on the road long before now." Yawning, arms overhead, she stretched. "Is the coffee ready?"

He had to chuckle between exclamations caused by shooting pains in his leg. "Ow, ooh, not good."

"It would have been much worse if you hadn't elevated it," Kaitlin assured him. "Let's get out and walk around a bit to limber up, then clear off the truck's silly decorations and get a move on."

"Hey, that's my bedding you're complaining about. It was a sacrifice for the cause."

"And fully appreciated," Kaitlin said. "It's just not something I care to haul across the state, flapping in the breeze." She opened her door and slid out. "I'll shake the twigs and what have you out of the outside blanket while you dump your lovely cedar bedding. If worse comes to worst we can gather more tonight."

He didn't like the sound of that. "Whoa. It shouldn't take us two days to cross the state. It's not that far."

"It will be if we take back roads and stay off the main drags. Highways are faster, sure, but they're also exactly what your enemies would expect. I say we fool them, cross to the opposite side of the lake the first chance we get and work our way around. The drive will be prettier."

"That's not a medical decision," he reminded her. "We'll go straight in."

Expecting plenty of argument, Daniel waited. Apparently, Kaitlin was silently capitulating because she just shrugged, scooted closer to the door on her side and climbed out. She was pulling branches off the hood when he started on the opposite side.

"Since you've been here before, where can I fill my gas tank?"

"I think I remember a couple of stations where Highway 65 crosses the lake. That goes toward Sedalia." He paused, visualizing the map. "Never mind. That'll be too far out of our way. We'll find something closer."

"Whatever. I still have almost half a tank. I just

didn't want to go on without planning for every possible glitch."

"Understood." Cautious, Daniel remained disturbed by her lack of argument. It wasn't like Kaitlin to give in so easily. Either she was no longer upset by his decision to head straight for St. Louis or something else was going on in that inventive brain of hers. No telling.

He didn't think she'd ever betray him, but he did assume she would defy his orders if she thought he was acting foolishly. When he was feverish and needed care, that was permissible. Now that he was back to his old self, however, it was not.

"I'll want coffee," Kaitlin said flatly, sliding behind the wheel. "Lots of it." She patted the dashboard as if the truck was a house pet. "Gas for the nice truck, coffee for the nice driver."

"Fine with me." He clicked his seat belt. "We may even find a place that has sandwiches or something."

"Truck stop sandwiches? Ewww. I'll pass. We have enough problems already."

"I've eaten lots of those sandwiches and never had a problem," he answered.

"Nuts and berries are safer."

The brief look she shot his way was troubling. "Kaitlin...what are you up to?"

He saw her hands tighten on the steering wheel before she replied. "I'm doing my best to get us out of this mess, that's what. My arm muscles are sore from driving, my back is stiff from sleeping sitting up and I have a pounding headache."

"In other words, I should shut up and leave you alone."

"Smart man."

"Okay. Hopefully you'll feel better after you've had some strong coffee." With the remembrance of the previous morning's weak drink he started to smile. "Not like what you made for me yesterday."

To Daniel's relief the corners of her mouth started to twitch. "You didn't seem to care for it."

"Understatement," he said, smiling fully and looking over at her. "It was by far the worst I have ever tasted."

"Well, at least it was memorable."

"Oh, yeah. And good for dousing the fire."

"I heard you do that but I let it slide. You should have seen your face when I handed you the cup. I was actually surprised you had the guts to taste it."

"I told you I was brave."

Slowing as they approached pavement, Kaitlin's grin faded. "You didn't have to tell me that," she said. "I've always known."

If they hadn't been at a literal crossroads he would have tried to come up with a witty reply. As it was, however, the situation didn't leave room for levity. Checking both ways he saw no traffic.

"Turn right," he said, "then keep an eye out for a sign that points to a tourist area. We'll find gas there."

"Gotcha."

"No questions? No argument? Is your headache that bad?"

Kaitlin made another face, and although she didn't divert her attention from the road ahead she spoke clearly. "If you must know, my worst headache is sitting right here next to me."

Given her mood, Daniel didn't laugh out loud when the urge hit him, although he wanted to. There were lots of things he wanted to do that he refused to consider. Things like patting her hand and telling her she was pretty despite her wrinkled outfit and beautiful, flyaway, corn silk–colored hair.

And then there was the hug he wanted to bestow, not to mention the kisses he'd already given her in his imagination. If reality turned out to be half as wonderful as he'd pictured it, he might even change his mind about real dating.

That's assuming he survived and Kaitlin agreed to start seeing him, he added, his emotions in turmoil. She would. She must. He wasn't going to just let her walk out of his life after all they'd been through.

But I should, he countered his own thoughts. A lot of crimes were going to have to be solved, their perpetrators arrested and sent to prison, before he'd feel safe opening his personal life to anyone. Nothing he wanted for himself was worth risking Kaitlin's becoming collateral damage the way his former partner, Levi Allen, had.

If only there had been someone else, anyone else, he could have asked for aid. His thoughts came full circle. Who would have done this much for him, have stuck with him as long as Kaitlin had? He couldn't think of a single person, friend or fellow officer, he trusted as much as he did this extraordinary young woman. Did she have a clue how special she was? Daniel doubted it.

The truck slowed and made a turn, jarring him from his reverie. "You saw a sign for gas?"

"And food, which means I can get my coffee," she said.

"I hope it helps your headache," Daniel said, meaning the pain in her head.

When Kaitlin's lips twitched and she said, "Oh, you're going to drink some, too," it took him a second to realize she'd made another subtle joke.

"Sounds like I'd better buy you the giant size."

"Whatever works. You're going to go inside?"

"I thought I would."

"Then you'll need this," she said, grabbing some crumpled bills out of her pocket right before pulling into an empty spot by one of the pumps.

Although he took the money, he grimaced. "I really hate this situation. You know that, right?"

She was smiling. "Yeah. Personally, I'm kind of enjoying the part where I get to be the boss."

"That figures. You'll probably be running the whole ambulance company by the time you're twenty-five."

"Then I'd better hurry," she replied, getting out and reaching for the pump nozzle. "If they want you to prepay, start with twenty so you get a little change back. I'll be in as soon as I'm done out here."

His answer was a wave. A lot of women might enjoy being in charge as much as Kaitlin did but few would come right out and admit it. With her, what you saw was the real thing. No pretense, no ruses to lead men on. That was beyond refreshing.

Opening the heavy glass door with little difficulty he headed for the back to freshen up before choosing food and drinks. By the time he hobbled to the coffee urn Kaitlin was already sipping from the largest cup available.

She handed him a plastic sack and a smaller cup of steaming coffee. "I didn't know if you drank it black or not so I put sugar and creamers in the bag."

"Okay, I'll just…"

"No," she said.

Daniel's first thought was that she was teasing.

Then he noticed how her eyes were scanning the little store. Something was bothering her. A lot.

She grasped his elbow, almost causing him to slosh coffee out the hole in the lid. "Come on."

"Okay, okay. I'm coming." He lowered his voice. "What's wrong? Did you recognize someone?"

"No. Just a creepy feeling. Trust me. We need to hit the road ASAP."

"How do you know...?"

Giving his arm a tug she shook her head. "I don't know anything for sure, okay? All of a sudden I got nervous so I came in to hurry you up."

"Maybe you don't realize what you did see but your subconscious does."

"Maybe. I don't really care."

By this time they were back out the door. Kaitlin had circled the truck and was getting in. Daniel threw his cane into the bed, handed her his coffee cup and hoisted himself into place.

As he did so he noticed several vehicles off to the side of the redbrick building. The morning air was cool enough to create visible clouds of exhaust, proving that the other cars were idling, not parked.

He canted his head. "Over there. Something about them looks fishy."

"Whatever." She dropped the truck into gear and pulled away from the bank of pumps.

Tourist vehicles clogged the Highway 5 intersection, keeping her from driving as fast as he knew she wanted to.

"Take it easy. We don't want to get in a wreck or hurt anybody."

"I know what I'm doing."

Daniel had been watching the service station behind them in the outside mirror. What he observed was disquieting, at best.

"I'm afraid you may have had a reason to be jumpy," he said. "One of those suspicious cars just pulled out behind us and the other one is in line after him."

If her old truck had been a military tank Kaitlin would gladly have climbed right over the traffic jam and squashed every troublesome car, truck and travel trailer as flat as a pancake. Good thing for all those clueless motorists that she was in a regular pickup.

Frustration took over. Letting go of the steering wheel she slammed her palms against it as if that would help. "Aargh!"

"Feeling better now?"

"No." If he laughed she wasn't going to be responsible for her actions.

"I gathered." He was leaning to see the reflection in the mirror better and sipping coffee as if nothing was wrong.

"How can you *do* that?"

"Do what?" He saluted with his paper cup. "Oh, this? It's a trick all cops learn sooner or later. Eat and drink whenever you get the chance because you never know how soon you'll get another opportunity."

The light ahead turned red, trapping them in the solid sea of cars. Eyeing her giant cup, Kaitlin decided there was no way she'd be able to handle it if they were racing down a winding road in flight or pursuit.

"I'll let you know when the light changes," Daniel said. "Enjoy your breakfast."

"All I need is this coffee. Whew! Hot."

"What's in the bag?"

When she glanced over at him he was checking for himself and hefting a paper-wrapped bun. "Looks like fried egg and mystery meat."

"Better than the freeze-dried pot roast, I hope."

"Has to be."

"Not necessarily." Seeing a narrow opening between two slowly creeping cars she whipped the wheel with her free hand and nosed in, thrusting her cup at Daniel. "Hold this."

He obliged. "Smooth move. Reminds me of the way you sneaked between those trucks at the clinic." He chuckled. "I didn't think you'd make it, then or just now."

"Never underestimate me," Kaitlin told him.

She reached for her coffee and he placed the cup in her hand while surrounding cars jockeyed for space to move forward.

Although she'd bought both sandwiches for her companion, she had to admit to hunger now that the odor of hot food was filling the cab. "That smells good. How does it taste?"

"A whole lot better than the pot roast."

"Good."

"Want a bite?"

"Can't. I'm driving with one hand as it is."

Scooting sideways he presented the sandwich. "Here. I'll hold it for you."

"Naw. I'm good."

"Good and hungry, I imagine," he countered. "C'mon. Be a sport. Let me do something for you for a change."

"Well, since you put it that way." Keeping her eyes on the road she leaned just far enough to reach the hot egg sandwich and took a big bite. "Um. That is good."

"Told you so. Oops. The light's changing."

Kaitlin was way ahead of him. Dropping her cup into one of the two round holders she put both hands back on the wheel. "Here we go."

Once through the main intersection she'd hoped they'd make better progress. When that didn't happen she decided on evasive driving and turned into the first business that looked promising.

"Where are you going?"

"Playing hide-and-seek. We should know in a few minutes whether or not those cars are after us."

"If they are, we'll be easier to overtake in parking lots."

"Not after I find an outlet on the opposite side."

"Suppose you don't."

"Then you'll have a reason to complain."

"Meaning I don't yet?"

"When you're right, you're right. Hang on to your coffee. And balance mine if it starts to tip over. Those holders aren't made for anything that size."

Bouncing over speed bumps sloshed coffee onto the white gauze of Daniel's bandage.

Kaitlin saw him jump. "Watch your leg. Keep it dry."

"Anything else? Would you maybe like me to do a handstand or somersault while balancing two cups of coffee and a half-eaten sandwich?"

"The bandage is most important. Pour my coffee out the window if you can't handle it."

"Not on your life," he shot back. "I'm keeping anything that might improve your morning mood."

A loud "Ha!" was her first reaction. Then she added, "I'm a lot sweeter when I'm not running for my life. Or for your life, come to think of it."

* * *

By putting his smaller cup into the holder and lifting Kaitlin's, Daniel managed a controlled chaos while they swerved in and out of three more parking lots. He assumed Kaitlin would have kept doing it if they hadn't run out of opportunities. Sooner or later, he was going to have to admit she was right. They were no longer being followed. Therefore, the so-called suspicious cars had either not been waiting for them to come out of the station or had lost track of where they'd gone.

He took one last peek behind, then cleared his throat. "Um, looks like you were right. Nobody's on our trail now."

"So I can finally slow down?"

"Please." All he could do was chuckle at her expression. "Save some of that wild driving for later, in case we need it."

"There's plenty more where that came from," she countered. "I'm actually surprised it's so easy. I'd never tried speeding before."

"Adrenaline helps," Daniel told her, hoping she'd take the warning to heart. "If you weren't agitated you wouldn't feel so powerful and in command. Trust me. I know."

"If you say so."

"I do. How about finding an easy place to pull off where the truck can't be seen from the road and finishing your breakfast." When he noted her reluctance he went one step further and confessed, "I wouldn't mind a short rest, either."

"And a pill," Kaitlin said with a frown. "You didn't take one early this morning, did you?"

"We were in kind of a hurry."

"We usually are," she said. "All right. I'll park behind that row of trash receptacles. Will that suit?"

Stinky, but a good choice otherwise. "Sure. Park. But keep the windows rolled up."

"Whatever you want."

What Daniel did want was to find someone, anyone, to take Kaitlin's place and drive him the rest of the way to his destination. Not only was that an impossible goal, she was irreplaceable in another way. Nobody could ever take her spot in his heart. Not even close.

He rubbed his knee below the bandage. Sheer determination might be enough to let him drive a short distance but there was no way he could take over from her and pilot a truck with a stick shift. If her truck had had an automatic transmission it would have been different. Then he could have dropped her off with the rest of the money and made the last leg of their journey by himself.

Knowing he'd have to be able to walk when he arrived, he stopped trying to think of ways to drive, as well. No way could he do both. Not until he'd healed more, and that wasn't going to happen quickly. Plus, the longer the delay, the greater the danger. Like right now.

Popping the antibiotic and a painkiller into his mouth he washed them down with coffee. Kaitlin was watching him as if she half expected him to turn around and spit the pills out. Instead of acknowledging her concern he handed her a fresh sandwich and picked up his own to take another bite.

Had she sensed any special intimacy when he'd fed her? he wondered. It had felt like a loving gesture to him. So had her amiable acceptance of what he'd offered. If he'd thought about it more carefully he'd have given her the other sandwich in the first place. It had simply seemed so natural to share his that he'd acted without a qualm.

As if she could read his thoughts, Kaitlin held out her sandwich. "Would you like half of this one? I'll share. I don't think I can eat it all."

"No, I'm good."

To his delight she smiled broadly at him and said, "Yeah, you are," leaving the interpretation up to him. Considering his own blossoming feelings toward her, he chose to believe she was paying him a subtle compliment. It was going to be such a relief when they were able to speak freely and share fondness openly.

Soon, he promised himself. *Soon*. And this time he refused to even entertain the opposite scenario.

His brain might keep insisting their future was iffy but that didn't mean he had to accept the concept.

Reality was bound to intrude on them soon enough, and when it did, he'd deal with it.

In the interim, he was going to enjoy a few precious moments filled with the possibilities of a happy future.

If he had anything to say about it, it would begin with Kaitlin North.

SEVENTEEN

If Kaitlin had been able to relax she wouldn't have hurried her meal and gotten back on the road so quickly. Unfortunately, she knew that the longer they stayed in one place, the greater the chances they'd be spotted. Yes, it was a big state compared to some, but Daniel's enemies knew where he had come from and had probably figured out where he was headed. That gave them a corridor in which to concentrate their search. Once they figured out he wasn't traveling Highway 44 they'd branch out and any sighting of her truck would lead them northeast. If they really had had a visitor near their makeshift camp last night, the killers might already have zeroed in on this area.

She knew he wanted to get to his chief as fast as possible. She was also positive that sticking to a main highway was foolish. How she would convince him she was right was another story. If they came in high, skirted Jefferson City, the state capital, then dropped down and crossed the Missouri River, they'd be close to their destination. The only other option was to backtrack and cut over to 44. In her opinion, that could be suicide.

"Where are you going?"

Ah, he'd finally noticed. Well, there was nothing to do but confess. "I'm taking you to St. Louis."

"By way of Iowa?"

"Of course not. I told you I planned to avoid highways. That's what I'm doing."

"No wonder you wanted more gas. How much wandering around in the boonies do you intend to do?"

"As much as it takes."

She heard him sigh, saw him shake his head. "No, Kaitlin. Just no. I understand what you're thinking but I disagree. The longer we're on the road the greater our chances of being spotted. Start working your way toward Jeff City. We can take 50 across. It won't be as fast as I'd like but it'll have to do."

That didn't sound bad so she nodded. "All right."

Sensing that he was staring at her, she arched a brow and glanced over at him. "What are you doing? Trying to guess my thoughts?"

"Thankfully, that's impossible. I'm pretty sure I wouldn't like whatever you're thinking right now."

"You might. I actually think the route you just picked is satisfactory."

"I only chose it because we're already so far off track."

She laughed lightly. "You may be. I'm right where I intended."

"You have a map or GPS I don't know about?"

"I looked at one on the wall at the service station and could see several workable possibilities. You just mentioned one of them. I'm good."

The set of his jaw and his crossed arms left no doubt he was upset, particularly with her. That was unfortunate but understandable. She'd cope. Incurring Daniel's displeasure was nothing compared to what she'd experienced when she'd informed her parents she was dropping out of medical school.

That decision was one she'd made for her own benefit and she was prepared to stick with it regardless.

This time, however, she was acting on Daniel's behalf and was not quite as sure of herself. Yes, she'd prayed about it, but that was no guarantee that her own ego hadn't usurped control and misdirected her well-intentioned choices.

Please, Lord, stick with us, with me, Kaitlin prayed silently. *You know my heart is in the right place. Help me help him.*

The urge to keep asking the same thing over

and over was strong so she persisted while she wondered how long it might be before God got tired of listening to her incessant babble.

"Mercy. I need mercy," she whispered, realizing her passenger might have overheard her.

A brief peek at him showed no change in his stiff posture. He was still giving off vibes of silent anger, which, considering the fact that he could be shouting at her instead, was the better of the two options.

She pressed the accelerator harder, taking the truck to the speed limit. They pretty much had the road to themselves except for a few slow-moving trailers and an RV that she passed easily.

The highway opened up ahead of her. There were still some twists and turns but nothing as sharp as they'd found in the Ozark Mountains. Her dependable old truck was chugging along, the sun was shining, the road was an easy drive and there was quiet in the cab, even if it had come at a price.

Sighing, Kaitlin relaxed her tense arms and pressed her back against the seat to ease the kinks in those overworked muscles. If the radio worked she'd play it, she mused, settling for humming the first gospel song that popped into her head.

Despite everything else, this promised to be a good day. A pleasant ride in mild fall weather. There were even trees still sporting bright autumn colors. They were passing a particularly pretty yellow and orange one. Kaitlin followed it with her eyes until she'd driven past, then tried to keep it in sight for few seconds more.

There it was. In the mirror. Until a curve in the road took it out of view.

And replaced it with a speeding, black SUV.

Her shout immediately startled him out of brooding. "Daniel! Behind us!"

"What? Where?" One look and he didn't need Kaitlin's answer. The problem was evident due to the other car's speed. "How long has it been there?"

"I—I'm not sure."

"Weren't you watching?"

"Yes, but just traffic in general. That last SUV we had trouble with was light colored. This one came out of nowhere."

"Can we outrun him?"

"I'm not sure. I hadn't shifted into overdrive so maybe. I've got the gas pedal all the way to the floor."

"He's gaining."

"I can see that. Is the gun still loaded?"

"Yes." In a swift, smooth motion he had it in his hand. "I won't shoot while we're moving. It's too hard to aim."

"But…"

"This is not a cop show on TV," he shouted,

freeing his shoulders from the upper part of the seat belt so he could swivel. "Without a straight stretch of road and no other cars anywhere near us I can't chance a shot. Even small calibers can still do damage over a mile away."

"Okay, I get it. Do you want me to pull over?"

"That's probably the worst thing you can do."

"Then what?"

Daniel could hear panic building in her voice, see it in the death grip she had on the steering wheel. *What, indeed?* Ideally, a state trooper would be parked along the road, waiting to stop speeders. And, as the old saying went, where was a cop when you needed one?

"Just keep driving. Maybe he'll make a mistake and spin out or something."

"That's not the dumbest thing I've ever heard but it's close," Kaitlin yelled.

"This isn't the time for jokes."

"Who's joking?"

Had Daniel been looking ahead instead of behind he would have anticipated an upcoming turn. At that speed it was almost too much for the truck. Tires squealed. Kaitlin screamed and hit the brakes just as the SUV behind them slammed into her bumper.

Momentum threw Daniel hard to the left. His leg twisted. Instantaneous agony made him cry out. The foam cooler on the floor kept him from bracing well with his good leg. Instead, his upper body landed against Kaitlin and she lost what little control she had left.

Instinct made Daniel grab for the wheel. She was screaming. At *him*.

The smoothness of the pavement ended. The pickup climbed a raised berm and became airborne. It seemed to hang suspended, like a dry leaf in the wind, then landed nose first and began to bump down a grassy slope dotted with cedars.

"Hang on!" Daniel yelled.

Kaitlin's "Let go!" came at the top of her lungs, ending with a wail that went on and on.

Bracing himself against the dash, Daniel knew it had been a reckless move to slip out of the top strap of his safety belt. The part of his psyche that had felt totally capable, totally in charge, had won out over common sense. If he lived through this he was never going to listen to that internal macho voice again.

Once he'd released the steering wheel Kaitlin was able to regain a smidgen of control. Seconds that were actually whizzing by seemed to pass at a crawl. Every time he started to think she had a handle on their plunge the pickup took another bounce. With the tires literally off the ground she had no brakes. No steering.

He had demanded they return to a highway. This was all his fault.

* * *

As Kaitlin fought for control she flashed back to her first ski run as a child. Her dad had insisted she'd be fine without more than a rudimentary lesson and had egged her on until she'd tried the simple slope. And fallen. Too bad she couldn't lean the truck the way she'd leaned her body on skis. Still, there was a certain rhythm to the descent that kept her from being totally frantic.

There was no time to do much except grip the wheel and pray. She had no idea when their plunge would end or how they'd stop. If it was against one of the sturdy cedar trees they were both going to be hurt, and so was her truck. They couldn't possibly flee on foot and succeed. At least Daniel couldn't. Not hurt the way he already was.

Hardly able to breathe let alone form a proper prayer, Kaitlin called out to her heavenly Father with her whole heart. They couldn't die like this. Not after all the other trials they'd come through.

Another bounce pushed the nose of the truck to the right. She turned the wheel. Got no response. Steering was gone. They might as well be in freefall. "Hang on!"

The way Daniel was braced against the dash she could imagine what would happen to his arms—and his head—if their vehicle stopped suddenly. What if they ended up badly hurt? They'd disposed of their only phone back at the lodge. There'd be no way to call for help.

Dark green boughs closed in on both sides of the pickup, slapping the windshield and scraping the paint. Kaitlin squeezed her eyes shut and covered her face.

The truck tilted. *Please, Jesus! Help!*

Tires on the high side left the ground. "No!" She wasn't ready to die in the middle of nowhere. She wasn't ready to die anywhere. She'd finally met a good, honest man whose off-beat sense of humor complemented hers and they were being tumbled like a pair of sneakers in a clothes dryer on their way to oblivion. That was so unfair.

Pain shot through her left shoulder as the seat belt tightened with a jerk. Everything was spinning. She didn't know up from down. "Daniel!"

Branches cracked outside her window. Glass shattered, raining down in tiny, blunted chunks the way its makers had intended. The truck bounced like a kid on a trampoline, each bounce less forceful than the one before.

Then, all was still except the cloud of dust swirling around them.

Dizzy, disoriented and suspended upside down, Kaitlin was almost afraid to look. "Daniel?"

He stirred. Moaned.

"Daniel!" She reached out to him, hoping to check his pulse. He was too far away to touch, but at least she could see his chest moving up and down. His breathing looked more normal than hers felt. Inhaling was difficult with the belt drawn so tightly across her chest. She coughed, struggled to release the catch. Although she didn't think she was hurt badly she was desperate to reach Daniel, to see if his lack of response was due to a serious or fatal injury.

Feet appeared outside her window. Someone in tennis shoes stopped and called out. More people gathered. A young man who looked like a teenager bent down and peered in at her. "You okay, lady?"

"I think so. Take care of my friend."

The rescuer straightened. "There's two of 'em. Alive. Call 911. And somebody bring me a knife to cut the seat belts."

Hearing him shout for aid calmed Kaitlin considerably. Anybody who wanted to call an ambulance could not be afraid of facing the authorities. State troopers would accompany a rescue squad, so that was additional proof they'd be safe. If she hadn't been so worried about Daniel she would have shouted with joy.

More helping hands reached for her. Kaitlin knew both she and Daniel should have their spines properly stabilized before they were moved but she could smell gasoline. The tank had been nearly full when they'd wrecked and must be leaking. Fire was a real danger.

Reaching as far as possible she managed to turn off the ignition before she was freed. Would that be enough to keep a spark from setting off the fumes?

Not willing to risk it, she let herself be dragged through the broken window and laid on the rough grass. Somebody held her down in spite of her struggles to rise. "No. Let me go. I have to see about Daniel."

"You need to stay still till the ambulance gets here," a kind-sounding voice explained.

"I'm an EMT. I know I'm not hurt. You have to let me go."

"Well, I don't know…"

Gathering strength as she breathed deeply she pushed the Good Samaritan away. "I've got this. Honest."

Strong men had removed Daniel from the wreck and two were carrying him up the hill toward the road. "Watch his neck. Keep traction," Kaitlin shouted after them.

By the time she caught up to the men and her beloved Daniel, Kaitlin was out of breath and coughing again. Her ribs were sore, likely from the safety belt, but other than feeling shaky she decided she was holding together.

Daniel stirred. Kneeling beside him she took

his face in her hands and told him, "Don't move. We were in a wreck. You could have spinal injuries."

His lashes fluttered. His eyes opened. In seconds she saw recognition. "You. Are you okay?"

"I'm fine." Flooded with relief she let herself weep, not that she could have held back all the tears of gratitude.

"Where are we?"

"Side of the road. My truck is toast but an ambulance is on the way. They won't come alone. We'll be safe."

Blinking rapidly, Daniel did exactly the opposite of what she'd told him to do. He levered himself into a sitting position.

"Lie down. Don't move. This is serious," Kaitlin said shrilly.

His gaze captured hers and held it for long seconds before moving to focus directly behind her. "Very."

A hand came to rest heavily on her shoulder. When she tried to duck away the fingers pinched enough to cause pain. She didn't turn. Didn't take her eyes off Daniel's face, hoping and praying she was wrong about his terse warning.

Another stranger appeared behind Daniel, looped his hands under his arms and assisted him to stand. "We'll take care of these folks," the figure announced to the crowd. "They can sit in our car until the ambulance gets here."

Kaitlin kept waiting for some bystander to speak up and insist they not be moved. No one said a word. When she studied the two burly men who had taken charge she understood why. Only a fool would argue with guys who looked like they could bench press a bus—and not break a sweat doing it.

Returning to making eye contact with Daniel she saw him sag and lower his eyelids as if he were about to pass out. Momentary fear gripped her until she saw him signal by refocusing on her, then winking before going back into the pseudo faint.

She feigned a swoon, too, hoping the captor behind her was aware enough to keep her from hitting the ground. As soon as she felt him grab her she collapsed completely and fell against him. Let her head loll. Became the human version of a rag doll as he picked her up.

"Put yours in the back seat," the man carrying Kaitlin said. "This one can go in with our gear."

"Not enough room," his companion replied. "You'll have to use the front seat or stack 'em like cordwood."

"Do we really care?"

Kaitlin couldn't believe they'd speak so revealingly in front of witnesses, yet neither seemed

bothered enough to shut up. Where were the police? What was taking so long? Had they wrecked
so far from a town with ambulance service that
medical aid would also be delayed? And what
in the world was Daniel up to? Personally, she'd
rather have walked under her own power than
submit to being carried by this brute.

Low, agonized groans were coming from Daniel. Kaitlin had to peek, had to know what was
going on. Her lids lifted enough to show her that
he now lay lengthways along the rear seat of the
SUV. If she hadn't seen him truly suffering during his fever-induced nightmare she might have
believed he was in actual distress now.

Their captors were apparently fooled because
one of them bent over him, listening, while the
one holding her asked, "What's he sayin'?"

"Can't make it all out. Sounds like he's babblin'
about something he left in the pickup."

"What?"

One of the curious bystanders started to back
away, then turned suddenly and ran down the
hill toward the wreck. That triggered the thug
to plop her onto the rear floor next to the seat
where Daniel lay and abandon her with her feet
hanging out the door. Others noticed their unusual
haste and joined them until half the motorists who
had stopped to assist were barreling back to the
smashed pickup.

A hoarse whisper prickled the hair on the back of Kaitlin's neck as it asked, "Did they both leave?"

There was no doubt who was talking. She lifted her head as little as possible to look. "Yes."

"Then I want you to slip out, circle around to the driver's side and get behind the wheel."

"We're stealing their car?" She was flabbergasted.

"Borrowing it. Unless they took the keys," he whispered. "Don't try to shut the doors. Once you get this running and pull away, the wind should take care of that."

"What about you? It's not safe. You might fall out."

Moving slowly, purposefully, Daniel slipped one arm through the shoulder strap of the nearest seat belt and wound it around his wrist and forearm, grasping it with both hands.

Kaitlin understood perfectly. She was already crouched down ready to go when she heard Daniel order, "Now. Before it's too late."

EIGHTEEN

Holding on to the strap with all his remaining strength, Daniel strained to pick out important sounds. Other traffic was still passing occasionally, but apparently enough cars had stopped to offer aid that later drivers were satisfied the situation was under control.

He wished he felt that way. As an officer of the law he had sworn an oath to protect every civilian. Unfortunately, he was in no position to do so at present and it galled him to have to leave the scene when kindhearted folks might be in danger. Sounds of sirens in the distance eased his mind some. Once troopers reached the scene he was sure the thugs would back off because they'd want to appear innocent and uninvolved.

Daniel lifted his shoulders without releasing the strap. "Are the keys in it?"

"Yes."

Tremors in her voice worried him so he said, "If it's an automatic, I can drive. The police are almost on scene. You can get out if you spot a patrol car."

"And leave you? Not on your life. I'm in this for as long as you need me." The engine roared to life. "Hang on. Here we go."

Even though he was expecting it, the speed of their acceleration took him by surprise, throwing him sideways against the back of the seat and straining his tenuous hold almost to the breaking point until Kaitlin got them back on the highway and straightened their course.

Her door slammed closed. The one by his feet did not. Although it was no longer flapping like the wing of a wounded crow Daniel was afraid it would attract too much attention so he sat up and slid across to try to close it.

"What are you doing?" she shouted over the whoosh of the air coming in and the wail of passing emergency vehicles.

"Almost got it. Just hold steady."

"I can handle it. Hang on."

"Wait!" Daniel had had to release the belt on the other side of the SUV in order to move closer to the unlatched door. The instant he realized what Kaitlin planned to do he made a grab for the only thing within reach—the door handle.

His weight pushed the whole door away instead of closed and he found himself hanging, head and shoulders outside the speeding car, feet and legs inside.

His "No!" was half shout, half scream. His fingers were slipping. His wounded leg was starting to give out. Pavement rushed by below, waiting to receive him face first if he failed to right himself.

Suddenly, the forces that had sent him sliding reversed. He brought the swinging door with him and heard the lock catch just as the last inch of his hold came loose.

"Are you okay?" Kaitlin was yelling above the squeal of tires against the asphalt.

Gasping, Daniel managed to pull himself onto the seat so she could see him. "I'm in. I made it. Keep driving. It won't be long before the guys who own this car report it stolen."

Instead of following his orders, she smoothly brought the SUV to a stop on the shoulder of the road. "I need..." she began before starting to cry.

"What? Go. Get us out of here."

"I can't see," she told him. "Can—can you drive?"

"Sure." Righting himself all the way and carefully positioning his sore leg, he opened the troublesome door and stepped out. Kaitlin was climbing over the center console when he slid behind the wheel and lifted his wounded thigh into place with his hands. All she said between sobs was, "I'm sorry."

Peace and self-assurance surged through Daniel as he took command. What a terrible choice he'd had to make when he'd abandoned those Good Samaritans. Yet he hadn't, had he? Other law officers were close by, which solved that problem but added another. If the thugs decided to report the theft of their vehicle immediately, he and Kaitlin might not get far before they were pulled over.

He gave her a look he hoped was encouraging. "Put your seat belt on."

"You, too."

Drawing it across his chest he had trouble finding the clasp. She leaned over and helped, her hand on his, her closeness another gift from God that he more than appreciated.

"Got it," she said, sniffling as she regained some control of her emotions. "I don't usually fall apart like that. I guess I'm overtired."

"We both are. It's been a wild morning." He chanced a smile in the hopes she was ready for a little teasing. "I can't say I'm too impressed with your trick driving, though. Let's not do that again, okay?"

She covered her face with her hands. "My poor truck."

"And your ID," he reminded her. "They'll have that from your purse and the truck license so they know where you live. It's a good thing you didn't decide to ditch me and go home."

"Not in a million years," she said, finally returning his smile while continuing to sniffle. "I wonder if they have any tissue in here."

"Take a look. We should check everything, anyway, just in case they left stuff we can use."

Daniel was keeping his eyes on the road, so he didn't watch her opening the center console but he couldn't miss her reaction. "Whoa."

"Did you find something to blow your nose with?"

"That's not all. Look."

A quick glance widened his grin. "Whoa is right. We've hit the jackpot." Not only had Kaitlin found cash and the tissues she needed, when she'd moved the items on top she'd exposed a handgun and a box of ammo.

"Don't touch that. Chances are it's tied to more than one crime and covered with incriminating fingerprints. I am glad to know it's in there. I just don't intend to touch it unless absolutely necessary."

"Gotcha." She blotted her damp cheeks and blew her nose. "I should have known the Lord would provide."

That brought a laugh. "You have a very strange mind, lady. You know that?"

"You can't prove God didn't have a hand in getting us a new vehicle."

"I suppose you're going to tell me He also

rolled us in a ball and threw us down that hill back there?"

"Well…"

"Uh-huh. That's what I figured. I can't believe He would condone what we had to do to get away, either. I'm sure not happy with it."

"Then why did we do it?"

"I saw no other options. If we'd hung around and told the troopers what was going on they either wouldn't have believed our story or they would have tried to arrest the guys from this car. A bunch of innocent bystanders could have been caught in a crossfire, including the folks who pulled us out of the wreck."

"Oh, my. I hadn't thought of that."

"We'll call it commandeering a vehicle for the benefit of stopping a crime," Daniel said.

"Will that get us out of trouble?"

He had to laugh. "Honey, we are so deep in this muddy mess it will take a battalion of lawyers driving heavy equipment to dig us out."

"But we're the good guys."

"Yes, we are." Had she noticed what he'd called her just then in a moment of carelessness? She wasn't acting as if she minded, was she? It was best to watch his speech more closely, though, so he didn't repeat any endearments. Not only were they not a real couple, they hadn't even dated.

Coming to a fairly straight stretch of highway

Daniel chanced a quick peek at Kaitlin. She'd shut the console and was looking away, keeping him from assessing her mood or well-being. "Kaitlin?"

"Um-hum."

"You okay?"

With a nod she turned her head. There was a broad smile on her face. Her blue eyes glistened like summer sunshine on ripples in a lake. Was she still fighting tears? He suspected she was and offered comfort. "You won't get in trouble. I'll make sure of it. I'll tell them I forced you if necessary."

"Won't work," she said.

"In a way it's the truth. None of this was your idea. Why won't it work?"

She blinked. Sniffled. Continuing to grin she patted the back of his hand before saying, "Because nobody will believe it. After all the time we've spent together I know better." Color rose in her cheeks. "You're a real sweetie, *sweetie.*"

Daniel was speechless. He told himself that was because he was busy driving and keeping his eye out for more threats. Well, he was. He was also struck dumb by Kaitlin's admission that she had not only heard his slip of the tongue, she was ready to reciprocate. He loved it. He also knew he should correct her mistaken notion immediately.

Instead, he schooled his features and gave her

a job designed as a distraction, hoping that was enough to keep her from pursuing the current conversation.

"Check the programming in the GPS on the dash and jot down any recorded destinations, will you? Then enter the address for my home station. I intend to go straight there."

"Won't the same kind of guys be waiting for you to do that?"

"Yes." He nodded. "We'll stop someplace on our way and buy different clothes. Disguises. It won't be foolproof but it may help one of us get through."

"One of us?"

Daniel was nodding as he spoke. "Yes. I'm going to write out a confession of sorts for you to give to Chief Broderhaven. Once he sees that, I expect him to arrange a way to bring me in safely. He's done it before, when he placed me in that safe house."

"The place where you were shot, you mean?"

"Not right away. I was there for months before anybody figured it out and came after me. My chief is totally trustworthy."

"So, according to you, that makes two of us, me and him."

There was nothing Daniel could do but nod. Kaitlin was right. He had no other proven allies on the inside. Although surely there were plenty, he didn't dare take the chance of placing his life in the wrong hands.

Was it safe to use Kaitlin as his messenger? he asked himself. Maybe. Probably. Unless the information from her truck reached St. Louis before they did.

Pressing harder on the accelerator he upped their speed. Even if they didn't stop to purchase disguises they might arrive too late. And there wasn't a thing he could do about it.

In spite of their race down the highway, Kaitlin was able to nap. The seats of the expensive SUV were much more comfortable than her truck had been, and considering the trials they had already passed through, she gave herself permission to close her eyes and rest.

Slowing speed and a change in direction roused her. "Why are we stopping?"

"I need to stretch," Daniel said, grimacing. "And you need to go shopping."

"After the gas and breakfast, we're broke."

"But our friends aren't." He lifted the lid of the console.

Her jaw dropped. "We can't touch that."

"I'll leave an IOU."

"For real?"

The soft sound of his laughter soothed her. "For real."

While she watched, he jotted a note on a scrap of paper from the pad she'd used to record the GPS addresses and exchanged it for some of the cash.

"I can't go into a store like this. Look at me."

"You look as if you camped in the forest then rolled down a hill in a wrecked truck, but otherwise I see no problems."

She knew his chuckle was at her expense. Crossing her arms she shook her head. "Nope. Ain't happening."

Daniel had pulled the keys, opened the driver's-side door and was slowly getting to his feet. "Would you rather stand out from the crowd in a store or attract attention in front of the police station we're headed for?"

Casting around for an alternative, any alternative, Kaitlin noticed the supplies in the rear of the SUV. She circled to the hatchback. "Pop this open and let's have a look. Maybe we won't have to waste time shopping."

"I can't believe I didn't think of this." He made a face. "You can stop showing me up anytime now."

"Why, when it's so much fun to outthink you?" *This is one of the things I love about you*, she admitted silently. *You can take a joke as well as deliver one.*

"Okay, just keep it private. I'd hate to have the reputation of being outsmarted by a woman."

"Hah!" She laughed lightly. "If I thought you were serious I'd take offense." Another giggle. "Anyway, it's too late."

"Probably." As she wiggled a heavy suitcase toward herself he took the handle and assisted. "As big as those two guys were, I doubt we'll find anything in here that fits."

"As long as it's clean I don't care if I swim in it," Kaitlin said. She rummaged through the clothing and held up a blue broadcloth shirt with long sleeves. "Oh, goodie. Big *and* tall. My kind of dress."

"You're kidding."

She held it up to her shoulders and checked the length. "Not in the slightest. It drops to my knees. Now all I need is a belt."

"In your size? Fat chance."

"*Fat* is the key word." A tan-colored web belt was rolled up and tucked into a side pocket. By starting in front and wrapping both ends around her waist to cross in the back, she was able to bring it back to buckle in front.

"Okay. Your turn." Kaitlin stepped back and scanned the parking lot. Nobody was paying the slightest attention to them. Impatient, she took out a plain white T-shirt and tossed it to Daniel before pointing across the street. "I'm going to go freshen up and change in that gas station rest-room. I'll probably be able to buy a comb and lip gloss there, too. Coming?"

"I'll drive over so we're close to the car for a getaway," he said.

"Suit yourself." She was already jogging away with her clean clothes. "I'm not waiting."

Soap. Water. Heaven, she thought. "I am so looking forward to this."

For a person whose habits included a daily shower and washing her hair, she was more than eager to feel clean again. If the restroom had a hot-air hand dryer she could even rinse out the clothes she wasn't able to replace and dry them that way. Oh, joy!

Thoughts of the products available to her in the big-box store where Daniel had parked intruded. She dashed them away. Speed was crucial. In her opinion, so was cleanliness and since she had the chance to wash she was not going to blow it.

A quick dash down the toiletries aisle bought her a brush, shampoo and scented hand soap. She tossed a twenty onto the counter. "I'll be back in a flash. Keep the change."

By the time she was done, a short line had formed outside the locked door. Kaitlin was beaming as she pushed past with apologies. "Sorry. Sorry."

She'd rolled up the sleeves of the shirt and

belted it as planned. A colorful scarf around her neck would have made the outfit look enough like a dress to have fooled most men and perhaps a few women. Even plain as it was, she was pleased.

An added plus was the expression on Daniel's face when she walked out and he saw her. The only thing better would have been sandals instead of her work shoes and she spotted a rack of flip-flops by the exit. There was also a touristy T-shirt that was perfect for him and since she could see he'd already bought food and drinks she simply scooped up her choices and paid for them.

"You bought a ball cap, too. Nice," Kaitlin said. "This shirt is for you. The white one makes you look as if you snitched it from your daddy."

"Only if Daddy was a big, green, muscle-bound monster who roared when he was mad," he said, picturing the Incredible Hulk.

"Works for me. Let's hit the road. If we drive with the windows open my hair will dry the rest of the way."

"And you'll freeze."

"So, I'll turn up the heater, too."

When Daniel gave a short chuckle and asked, "Do you have an answer for everything or is it just my imagination?" Kaitlin was more than ready.

"As long as you don't require me to be right all the time, I have an answer for everything."

NINETEEN

They had traded driving duties again and Kaitlin was at the wheel by the time they passed the city limits and caught a glimpse of the famous St. Louis arch in the distance. The GPS in the SUV piloted them through a series of interchanges, indicated which off-ramp to take and guided her along the unfamiliar city streets while Daniel went over his plan again, amending it as he talked.

"I've changed my mind. Just drop me off. I'll go in while you wait outside."

"Hey, I didn't get all dressed up to sit this one out," she gibed. "I even bought new shoes."

"A bargain at less than five bucks, too."

"I'm thrifty, especially when I'm spending hot money."

Sobering, Daniel tried to dial back her enthusiasm by citing cold facts. "This isn't a TV show, Kaitlin. These bullets are real. All you have to do is look at my leg if you want proof."

"I know that. I also know I'm doing the right

thing," she said firmly. "I can't tell you how, I just know, okay?"

"That's a pretty shaky basis for infiltration into enemy territory."

"Most of them aren't enemies. You said so yourself. All I have to do is dodge the sneaky ones and deliver a note to your chief. What could be easier?"

"Just about anything." When he reached across to touch her hand and felt her shiver it shook him, as well. "I don't want you to risk it."

"Too late."

"It's never too late."

"Remember you said that when this is over." He saw her cheeks growing more rosy before she said, "I don't want to lose you, Daniel."

"Of course not. I want us to continue being friends, too," he said, assuming that was what she wanted to hear. Eyes flashing, she gave him a look that proved how wrong he was. Daniel rallied. "What? You don't see us as friends? I sure do."

"Fine. I guess it beats getting a dog."

"Who put the sour lemon drops in your coffee?"

"Nobody." Kaitlin was pulling to the curb at a bus stop that happened to be empty at the time. "The navigation system says we're five hundred feet from our destination. You wanted me to let you out early so you could walk up, right?"

"Right. This is close enough. Hang on to the let-ter I wrote to Chief Broderhaven in case you need proof of your innocence. I'll approach on foot so I don't stir things up any more than necessary."

Kaitlin lowered the power windows as soon as he'd slammed the door. "You can do as you please but I'm still going to see your chief and tell him everything."

"No. This is police business. I make the rules, remember?" The stubborn set of her jaw and flashing of her eyes was more than worrisome. It was frightening. He grasped the door frame with both hands. "My way, Kaitlin."

"Uh-uh. Not this time."

"I thought we were friends," Daniel said, hoping that approach would sway her.

Immediately before she pulled away and left him standing there by the curb she looked him straight in the eye and said, "If that was all you were to me I might listen."

Knowing she had revealed too much, yet certain the clue to her deeply felt commitment had sailed right over his head, Kaitlin forged through traffic. She could see him reflected in the side mirror, struggling along in his black ball cap and the tourist shirt that fit so well it set off his muscular arms and chest. The sight melted her heart and nearly weakened her conviction.

Then she recalled all the things he'd told her

about his complicated situation. The most important detail was the danger of being assassinated. She didn't care who fired the bullet or wielded the knife. All she cared about was keeping Daniel alive.

Yes, she was being selfish. She wanted her dreams for them as a couple to be fulfilled. But even if he never learned to care for her as much as she cared for him, that was okay. Loving him, she only wanted the best, whatever brought him happiness. That was what her parents had never understood, wasn't it? When you really, truly loved someone, you had to put their happiness first, even if it wasn't in line with your own vision.

Her jaw clenched. So did her hands on the wheel. There was no place to park in front of the police station or at the jail next door. The only way she'd beat Daniel in the door was to leave the enormous SUV double-parked.

She eased against the side of a patrol car at the curb. They needed this vehicle as proof of one of the attacks on Daniel, if not more, so she had to ensure that it wasn't stolen. Climbing out, she locked the doors behind her, hooked the keys through her belt and ran up the stairs into police headquarters.

The lobby was busier than the street had been. Casting around for signage, she was accosted by an old man who reminded her of Barney, the surprising helper from Mags's clinic.

Swallowing past the lump in her throat, Kaitlin forced a smile. "Hi. Can you tell me how to find Chief Broderhaven?"

He cackled. "Oh, they'll find you if they want you, sweetheart. What'd you do? Sell fake Girl Scout cookies?"

Kaitlin dodged him and waded into the crowd. Surely one of these people knew his or her way around the station well enough to give directions. All she had to do was pick out a friendly face and ask before Daniel arrived and stopped her.

She'd spent her adult life teaching herself not to judge people by the way they dressed or acted but now she had to set that aside. One by one she scanned the gathered crowd. Some seemed agitated, others surprisingly calm. Her gaze paused on a sensibly dressed, middle-aged woman who was seated in one of the chairs along a wall. Her hair was short but not spiked, her slacks and top a matching sea green. A tote bag sat at her feet. Yellow yarn led from the bag to the knitting in her lap.

Kaitlin had made her choice. She approached and would have sat next to the woman if there had been an empty chair. "Excuse me. I wonder if you can help me."

The woman looked up, not at all startled, and smiled. "Certainly. If I can."

"Thanks." Kaitlin licked her lips and kept her hand pressed to her side, subconsciously guarding the note she carried. "I need to find my way to the chief's office. Chief Broderhaven?"

"I'm sure that's upstairs, dear." The woman pointed with a knitting needle. "Elevators are over there."

"What floor?"

"Oh, dear. I have no idea." She elbowed the scruffy-looking youth seated next to her. "Do you know?"

"Yeah, sure. I can show her." He pushed to his feet.

"That's not necessary. I can find it myself." Kaitlin was nervous for good reason. She was out of her element and floundering. Unfortunately, when she looked back to the knitter for moral support, she saw the same kind of predatory expression the youth had. "Um, thanks, anyway."

His thin fingers made a grab for her wrist. She shook him off just as she had the old man. That created a fuss that brought a uniformed officer to her side.

He stepped between Kaitlin and the unruly youth. "Okay, everybody settle down."

She thought she was safe until the officer turned and saw her face. He seemed surprised, as if he recognized her, except that was impossible, wasn't it? He blinked twice. Took her by the elbow and tried to lead her away.

Panicky, Kaitlin whipped away from him. "Let go of me. I didn't do anything wrong. I was just asking for directions."

The uniformed man paused to study her. "Where did you want to go, ma'am?"

"I need to see the chief. It's important. Really." She was beginning to think she had convinced him when he nodded and started to guide her away again. Her sense of accomplishment vanished as they reached a side hallway and another man fell into place directly behind her.

They had her boxed in. Trapped. Still, there was an outside chance they were escorting her to Broderhaven. She squared her shoulders, lifted her chin and tried to appear composed.

That worked until the man following her said, "Welcome to St. Louis, Ms. North. We've been expecting you."

Daniel reached the station's front steps and managed to climb them without too much discomfort. Once he had realized what Kaitlin was up to and had done his best to run, endorphins had kicked in and helped dull his pain.

He pulled open the front door and prepared to enter just in time to see Kaitlin being escorted away. Had she succeeded? Was she being taken to Broderhaven? He wished he knew.

What Daniel wanted to do was knock aside every person in his way and grab her. Stop her. Take her place. Logically, his chances of doing that were less than zero. A quick scan of the crowd lowered those chances even more. Several of the men loitering in the lobby were familiar to him. If they spotted him there his life would end immediately and bystanders would likely pay a high price, too.

He ducked his head, masking his face with the brim of his baseball cap, and let the door close as he backed away. His heart was torn. A dead man wasn't any good to Kaitlin. Staying alive came first. Then he'd do whatever was needed, even if it meant trading himself for her and going to Glory that way. At least it would be noble.

In his mind he imagined Kaitlin grinning at him and telling him it would also be stupid. She'd say that for sure. And he agreed, up to a point. If it came down to his life or hers, however, she was going to survive. No matter what he had to do.

The height and depth and strength of his convictions told Daniel far more than he'd expected. No wonder she had acted upset when he'd suggested that their relationship was that of mere friends. Somehow, in the space of a few hectic days, he had fallen in love with her and she with him. This was no childish crush, either. Their extensive time together had led to a closeness he had not experienced with any other woman.

"And I haven't even *kissed* her," Daniel muttered, more than a little put out with himself, yet thankful he hadn't spoiled his chances for loving expressions of affection later, when the time was right.

Holding remembrances of Kaitlin close he made his way toward the jail next door. That building also faced the street with a wide alley between it and police headquarters. By stationing himself at that junction he'd be able to watch both the front door of the station and most of the activity to the rear.

And he'd also blend in, he realized as he studied the relatives and friends awaiting either release of or information about incarcerated loved ones.

Daniel's polite nod to a poorly dressed, deeply tanned older man wearing overalls and a hat like his was returned with a smile. "Name's Jim, Jimbo if you was to ask my mama." He stuck out a gnarled hand.

They shook. "I'm Dan."

"Pleasure. Is yours comin' or goin'?"

"Pardon?" Daniel saw Jim raise a brow and nod toward the jail to clarify. "Ah. Neither. She's in the police station. It's a long story."

"Ain't they all?" Jim chuckled noisily.

Although he didn't take his eyes off the alley, Daniel was greatly relieved to have someone to talk to. "Yeah. Only mine's innocent."

Another low chuckle. "Like I said…"

Daniel had to smile. "I know what you mean. But Kaitlin really is innocent. She got sucked into trouble by helping me out after I got hurt."

"Your leg?"

"Yeah."

"Reminds me of Desert Storm. I was sure a mess after goin' through that, I'll tell you. Thought I'd never get a good night's sleep again." He lowered his voice to speak more privately. "Some of my buddies never did recover."

"I've heard. I'm sorry."

Jim shrugged. "Hey, what is, is. Can't go back and change anything." Hesitating, he looked at Daniel so steadily it unnerved him enough to grab his attention. "You right with Jesus, son?"

Although he'd never heard it asked quite that way, Daniel nodded. "Yes. I'm a believer. So is Kaitlin."

"Good to hear. I couldn't have made it without God in my corner."

"I know what you mean," Daniel told him. "I just hope He's looking after her now."

"Course He is."

"She's in a pretty tough spot."

"You either trust Him or you don't," Jim said.

"If she's in the police station you got nothin' to worry about."

Daniel rolled his eyes. "You have no idea."

Leaning against the brick wall and producing a smile that crinkled his already lined face, Jim nodded. "I'm a good listener if you feel like talkin' about it."

Refocusing on the rear of the station to keep watching for Kaitlin, Daniel began to relate the complicated story. By the time he was finished his new buddy was patting him on the shoulder in commiseration.

"That's a doozy of a tale, son."

"It's all true."

"Too bad. What's your next move?"

"Don't know. I can't storm the station and get her out, and unless I can talk to my chief, I'm stuck."

"Maybe I can get in to see him. Tell him you're waitin' out here. And see about the girl."

"You'd do that?"

"It'd be kinda like helpin' my boy." He jerked his chin toward the jail. "He's in there so often he's probably got a room named after him."

Daniel gave a monstrous sigh. "All right. We need to find a pencil and paper so I can write a note to prove I sent you."

"I got a bail bondsman's card right here. Will that do?"

"Sure. See if you can borrow a pen." As he turned back to the alley Daniel gasped and shouted, "No!"

"What's up?"

"There." Daniel pointed. "That's Kaitlin. They're putting her in a patrol car."

"Want me to stand in the way and stop em?"

"No. They'll run you down." Staring at the double-parked SUV he saw a traffic officer working to gain access. "We could take that if I hadn't told her to lock the doors."

"I got a truck," Jim said. "She ain't much but she'll do unless they hit the highway. She blows blue smoke if I push her too hard."

Daniel felt as if he were hanging on to his self-control by a fraying thread. "Where is it?"

"'Round the corner. You wait here. I'll can make better time if you don't try to keep up with that bum leg."

The roar of a powerful engine echoed down the alley. Daniel had to take a step back to keep the white patrol car from sideswiping him. Two officers shared the front seat.

Wild-eyed and more frightened than he'd ever seen her, Kaitlin stared out at him through a rear window. Her lips were moving. It actually looked as if she was saying, *I love you.*

Daniel was lost. Hopeless. Destroyed by the thought he might never have a chance to tell her he loved her, too.

TWENTY

Kaitlin couldn't believe she'd fallen into this trap so easily. Taught to trust men in uniform, she'd failed to act soon enough, to raise a fuss in public when she'd had the chance. Doing that might not have helped but it was better than simply letting herself be led away, meek as a lamb.

Still, she refused to believe Daniel had been wrong about her intelligence and courage. Maybe she'd been relying too heavily on his expertise in law enforcement and not enough on her own wits. Whatever had led her to this moment, this predicament, she knew there had to be a way out. There had to be. She was not spending the last moments of her life in the presence of men like these.

"So," she said, managing to sound a lot more nonchalant than she was, "what's plan B?"

Neither answered.

"Oh, come on, guys. I figured it wasn't good when you grabbed me back there but we can work something out."

The man in the passenger seat turned his head slightly. "You have no idea what kind of trouble you're in, do you?"

"Sure. I stole a car. Big deal. The owner of that SUV wrecked my truck. Did you expect me to walk home?"

Seeing the two men make eye contact across the patrol car's equipment console was encouraging. If they believed she was on the same side of the law they were, she'd be in a better position to survive. The hardest part was figuring out what to say without actually lying. A quick but heartfelt, "God, forgive me," came out sounding like a breathy sigh.

Although handcuffed, Kaitlin was able to swivel enough to peer through the rear window. There was no sign they were being pursued. No hope of help. No sign of Daniel.

If her captors got too far ahead he'd never be able to find her. If only…

Kaitlin stopped herself. Her time for outwitting their adversaries was apparently coming to an end, like it or not.

"Well, I don't like it," she said aloud, feeling a tiny surge of courage that she hadn't realized lingered.

When her captors both laughed they made her angry.

"If I were you I'd be worried," she said, growing stronger by the second. "You may think Daniel Ryan is done but I assure you, he isn't. He never will be if anything happens to me. You got that? He's connected in ways you can't imagine."

Her reference was to his Christian faith but when the statement came out sounding threatening in an earthly way she let it stand.

"'Yea, though I walk through the valley of the shadow of death, I will fear no evil; for Thou art with me,'" she quoted in a whisper, claiming it as a promise. "'Thy rod and thy staff they comfort me.'"

Recalling the handmade cane Daniel had left behind in her truck made her wish she possessed something similar. There was no way to knock her captors over the head through the protective grill between the front and rear seats, of course, but she'd feel better if she had a weapon to fight back with. Sadly, she didn't.

Which left the source of power and support she knew was most important to begin with. God. And Prayer. She had seen amazing things happen during the past few days, things for which she had given thanks. No situation was hopeless. She just wished her heavenly Father had let her in on His plans ahead of time.

Daniel perched on the edge of the torn seat, bracing himself while Jim did his best to speed through the busy streets. The concept of speed and Jim's truck, however, were incompatible. If this was the best they could do, Kaitlin was doomed. Not only was the engine more sputter than roar, they were leaving a roiling cloud of blue and gray smoke in their wake.

Hang in there, Kaitlin. Don't give up, he kept thinking, wishing he could say it to her face.

Irony intruded in the person of Jim. "Some rescue squad you and I are, huh, buddy? Do you see her?"

"No. I was hoping this heavy traffic would slow them down. They may have turned off."

"Want to keep going?"

"I don't know."

"Well, at least we're on the right team," Jim said. He was weaving in and out of traffic, leaving a smoky wake that temporarily obliterated vehicles behind them. "Whoa! Flashing lights up ahead. Looks like a roadblock."

"See if you can get around it without drawing attention," Daniel said. "Otherwise we'll be forced to stop."

"It's not lookin' good, buddy. Sorry. I got no place to go except forward."

If Daniel had clenched his teeth any harder they'd have cracked. The urge to jump out and try to chase down Kaitlin on foot was strong. It was also foolhardy. His leg was too sore to support him for long, and if he fell he'd attract even more attention, something he must avoid at all costs.

"State troopers," Jim deduced. "I see their hats."

The line of waiting cars wasn't moving. Daniel decided to step out and join several other motorists who had done the same. One of them was monitoring breaking news on a cell phone.

"Do they say what's up?" Daniel eyed the phone.

"Something about a stolen car and escaped fugitives." He displayed the screen. Reflections of sunlight distorted the pictures but the audio was clear.

"…along Highway 44, earlier today. The suspects are described as a blond young woman and her male companion. Both are presumed armed and may be injured. Authorities are withholding their names until positive identifications can be made."

The search was for him and Kaitlin. *Now what?* If he was arrested he'd lose any chance of rescuing her before the gang used her as a surrogate to take the punishment meant for him.

Pacing nervously he started back along the line of idle cars, then reversed and rejoined Jim. "It's me they're looking for," he said through the open side window. "Me and Kaitlin."

"Then maybe they'll catch and hold her for you. State cops should be okay, right?"

"I guess so."

As lanes merged, a delivery van pulled into line three spaces ahead. Unable to see past it enough to be certain the roadblock really was a godsend, Daniel started to work his way forward on foot.

As he passed the driver's side of the van he gasped. Faltered. Almost dropped to his knees.

The patrol car carrying Kaitlin was up there, all right. And inching along. It was almost to the barricade. If the driver used his official status to pass through, Kaitlin was doomed.

Hitching every other step, Daniel began to run, not for his life, for *hers*.

How convincing did she need to be to get herself out of this? Kaitlin wondered. One thing was for sure. She needed to speak up as soon as her captors rolled down the window to talk to the officers working the roadblock.

She waited. Poised. Ready. Hardly able to swallow through her cottony throat. She'd only get one shot at this. It had better be good.

The uniformed driver opened his door and stepped out. Kaitlin mustered a scream of "Help! Help me!" before he slammed it behind him and went to converse with the trooper.

The passenger with her laughed. "Save it, lady. You're not the first prisoner who kept hollering how innocent she was. They're not gonna pay attention."

If only she could wave or give some kind of distress signal. They were less than fifteen feet from the checkpoint with only two cars ahead of them.

Assuming that her captor was delivering an explanation for his presence and planning to pass through without stopping again, Kaitlin's spirits plummeted. All she could do at this point was bang on the windows or shout when she was closer. The way things looked, her captor was right. Efforts as feeble as those were bound to be ignored.

And then she saw him. He never slowed, never looked aside to check on her, yet she knew exactly who was limping past. Somehow, Daniel had found her and was on his way to end this nightmare.

As long as her kidnappers didn't notice him in time to interfere, he had a good chance of making it all the way to the troopers.

Clasping her hands and throwing herself on the mercy of her heavenly Father, Kaitlin began to pray for all she was worth. Tears rolled down as pleas rose up. Specific words were less important than the condition of her heart, her wounded spirit. She was counting on her Savior for His promised intercession.

Realizing it was out of her hands she began to whisper, "Thank You, Jesus," over and over.

The driver returned. The patrol car started to roll forward.

Kaitlin refused to concede defeat.

"That's right," Daniel was telling one of the men at the barricade. "Chief Broderhaven can vouch for me." He pointed. "The woman in the rear of that unit is being kidnapped. She's not an official police prisoner."

It was all he could do to stop trying to explain and let the other lawmen puzzle it out. As long as they had doubts they'd have to act.

One of them left the line and returned to his car. Daniel watched him using his radio. Although he appeared no less confused when he came back, at least he wasn't laughing.

"The sergeant says to take charge of this guy and the other prisoner and hold everybody until he can sort this out."

Daniel presented his wrists to be cuffed. "Good idea. I think it would also be smart if you checked the IDs on those cops who have my friend, Kaitlin."

"We can do our jobs," the younger trooper blurted.

The more seasoned officer, however, was nodding. He rested his palm on the grip of his pistol as he sauntered up to the city unit and motioned for the occupants to get out.

Daniel held his breath. Resistance leading to an armed confrontation was the last thing he wanted.

The front car doors swung open. Two burly men exited. Now that Daniel could see their faces clearly he realized that at least one was an impostor. Apparently the trooper in charge had come to the same conclusion because he cuffed the driver while signaling to his partner to secure the other man.

The rear door popped open. Kaitlin clambered to her feet. Met his gaze. And ran straight into his arms.

All Daniel could do was loop his joined hands over her head and hold her. Words failed him, even words of comfort. This was the beginning of the end.

This was also the beginning of a new beginning, providing he didn't mess it up. He couldn't tell if she was crying or laughing or just gasping for breath. It didn't matter as long as she was safe—and stayed that way.

As they were escorted to a waiting state vehicle he asked, "Did you speak with Broderhaven?"

"My commanding officer just did. I'm supposed to take you into custody—for your own protection." Pausing beside his car, the trooper removed both sets of handcuffs then held the door open for them. "Hop in. I'll be back ASAP."

Sliding across the seat, Kaitlin gave him so little room he barely fit. That was a good sign. A very good sign. She also leaned into him as soon as he slipped his arm around her shoulder. "Are you okay?"

"I am now." She joined in the embrace. "I was afraid you'd lost track of me."

"I had. If we hadn't stumbled into this road-block…"

"We?"

"Yeah. I met another old boy like Barney. This one, Jim, volunteered to drive me."

Snuggling closer, Kaitlin sighed, then chuckled softly. "I guess one of those names will do, but I really wish you'd made friends with somebody like a Kurt or Justin."

"Why?" Totally puzzled, Daniel hooked a finger under her chin and raised her face so he could look into those amazing blue eyes while he tried to figure her out.

A blush rose. She grinned up at him. "Because," Kaitlin drawled, "I intended to name our firstborn son after one of the strangers who was so wonderful to us."

Daniel choked. Coughed. Finally regained his senses. "I—I haven't even proposed yet and already you're naming the kids?"

"Oh, I'm in no hurry," Kaitlin said. "We have a lot of little details to work out, such as making sure no more hit men are lurking in the bushes, but we will. I know we will."

"Pretty sure of yourself, aren't you?"

"Um-hum."

She leaned in closer. Daniel dipped his head. His lips brushed hers, then settled as if they had always belonged there. Life with this woman was going to be an adventure, all right, but he was more than ready for it to begin.

And judging by the way she was kissing him back, Kaitlin was, too.

EPILOGUE

Kaitlin had returned to Paradise and finished her paramedic studies by the time Daniel was ready to relocate. She'd spoken to the police chief in her little home town and a position was waiting for him. That left only his personal safety to worry about.

When he attended her paramedic badge-pinning ceremony he brought the news they had both been waiting for.

"The Feds raided the gang's headquarters just outside St. Louis and were met with armed resistance."

"Oh, no!" She slipped her arms around his waist.

"It's not that bad for law enforcement but the leaders who had put out the contract on me are out of the picture. I guess they figured dying in a shootout was better than going to prison for the rest of their lives."

"It's really over?" she asked, sounding both relieved and doubtful.

"It's really over. And I haven't had any nightmares since I decided to move to your hometown." Daniel gave her a kiss before he added, "So, are you ready to marry me?"

"We've had almost a year to really get to know each other. You haven't changed your mind, have you?"

"No. Have you?"

She stepped into his embrace. "No way."

He held her close. "The only thing that bothers me is those boys names you mentioned, honey. When we do decide to start a family, do you suppose you'd reconsider?"

Cupping his cheeks she looked up at him with a grin and a mischievous twinkle in her eyes. "Sure. Besides, all twelve kids may be girls."

His jaw dropped. "Twelve? Twelve, really?"

Kaitlin was laughing so hard she didn't act as if she'd heard a word he said. That was his Kaitlin. His future wife. His beloved. Life with her was certainly not going to be dull.

* * * * *

Dear Reader,

I come from a family filled with firefighters, EMTs, paramedics and nurses. My stint as an EMT was a short one but it taught me a lot about the rigors of that life. As Kaitlin and Daniel observed in this story, it takes a special kind of person to put themselves out for others, over and over again, with no expectation of reward or praise. They burn out. They struggle against unmerited guilt for failing to save every victim. They remember years later what a suffering child may have said to them in the midst of a terrible wreck and it haunts them.

So the next time you see or hear an emergency vehicle, please stop and pray for the ones aboard and the people they are racing to help. And if you harbor any doubts about your prayerful connections to the Lord, start by asking Him to accept you into His, into our, family.

I love to hear from readers! Visit me at my website, ValerieHansen.com, or email me directly at Val@ValerieHansen.com.

May you be blessed and thankful for it every day.

Valerie Hansen

Get 4 FREE REWARDS!

We'll send you 2 FREE Books plus 2 FREE Mystery Gifts.

Love Inspired® books feature contemporary inspirational romances with Christian characters facing the challenges of life and love.

FREE
Value Over
$20

Get 4 FREE REWARDS!

We'll send you 2 FREE Books plus 2 FREE Mystery Gifts.

Harlequin® Heartwarming™ Larger-Print books feature traditional values of home, family, community and—most of all—love.

FREE Value Over **$20**

THE FORTUNES OF TEXAS COLLECTION!

18 FREE BOOKS in all!

Treat yourself to the rich legacy of the Fortune and Mendoza clans in this remarkable 50-book collection. This collection is packed with cowboys, tycoons and Texas-sized romances!

YES! Please send me **The Fortunes of Texas Collection** in Larger Print. This collection begins with 3 FREE books and 2 FREE gifts in the first shipment. Along with my 3 free books, I'll also get the next 4 books from The Fortunes of Texas Collection, in LARGER PRINT, which I may either return and owe nothing, or keep for the low price of $5.24 U.S./$5.89 CDN each plus $2.99 for shipping and handling per shipment*. If I decide to continue, about once a month for 8 months I will get 6 or 7 more books but will only need to pay for 4. That means 2 or 3 books in every shipment will be FREE! If I decide to keep the entire collection, I'll have paid for only 32 books because 18 books are FREE! I understand that accepting the 3 free books and gifts places me under no obligation to buy anything. I can always return a shipment and cancel at any time. My free books and gifts are mine to keep no matter what I decide.

☐ 269 HCN 4622   ☐ 469 HCN 4622

Name (please print)

Address   Apt. #

City   State/Province   Zip/Postal Code

Mail to the **Reader Service:**
IN U.S.A.: P.O. Box 1341, Buffalo, N.Y. 14240-8531
IN CANADA: P.O. Box 603, Fort Erie, Ontario L2A 5X3